## *"I want you, Lesley," he whispered*

"I want you more now than I did when you were standing under the apple tree with blossoms floating around you."

She was bathed in disappointment, immersed in confusion. "Then why am I over here, and you're over there?" With trembling fingers she pulled the sheet up to her shoulders.

"Because I've decided to stop being selfish."

"I don't understand." Lesley flicked her heavy mane of hair over her shoulder, trying to hide her hurt expression.

Travis reached over and brushed the hair away from her face. "You're not ready for this," he whispered. "We both know it, but I've been trying to ignore it all night."

"I was willing. I am willing."

"Part of you is. But you need more than I can give you tonight."

Dear Reader,

Although our culture is always changing, the desire to love and be loved is a constant in every woman's heart. Silhouette Romances reflect that desire, sweeping you away with books that will make you laugh and cry, poignant stories that will move you time and time again.

This year we're featuring Romances with a playful twist. Remember those fun-loving heroines who always manage to get themselves into tricky predicaments? You'll enjoy reading about their escapades in Silhouette Romances by Brittany Young, Debbie Macomber, Annette Broadrick and Rita Rainville.

We're also publishing Romances by many of your all-time favorites such as Ginna Gray, Dixie Browning, Laurie Paige and Joan Hohl. Your overwhelming reaction to these authors has served as a touchstone for us, and we're pleased to bring you more books with Silhouette's distinctive medley of charm, wit and—above all—*romance*. I hope you enjoy this book, and the many stories to come.

Sincerely,

Rosalind Noonan
Senior Editor
SILHOUETTE BOOKS

# EMILIE RICHARDS
## Gilding the Lily

*Silhouette* *Romance*

Published by Silhouette Books New York

**America's Publisher of Contemporary Romance**

SILHOUETTE BOOKS
300 E. 42nd St., New York, N.Y. 10017

Copyright © 1985 by Emilie Richards McGee

Distributed by Pocket Books

ISBN: 0-373-08401-3

First Silhouette Books printing December 1985

10 9 8 7 6 5 4 3 2 1

America's Publisher of Contemporary Romance

Printed in the U.S.A.

Books by Emilie Richards

Silhouette Romance

*Brendan's Song* #372
*Sweet Georgia Gal* #393
*Gilding the Lily* #401

## EMILIE RICHARDS

grew up in St. Petersburg and attended college in northern Florida. She also fell in love there and married her husband, Michael, who is her opposite in every way. "The only thing that we agreed on was that we were very much in love. We haven't changed our minds about that in the sixteen years we've been together." They now live in New Orleans and have four children, who span from toddler to teenager.

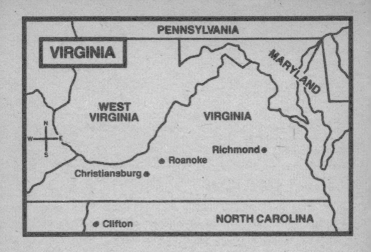

# Chapter One

The ancient blue pickup chugged slowly over the steep hill as if it, like its only occupant, was seriously considering permanent retirement. The farmer inside shook his head, his mouth twisting into a wry grin at the scene he was presented with. A tan Pinto was jacked-up by the side of the narrow, winding mountain road, and a young woman dressed for almost anything except changing a tire was in the process of trying to loosen the lug bolts on the left rear wheel of the car. With a resigned sigh, the old man pulled the truck onto the narrow rocky shoulder opposite her car and climbed down out of the cab, the slam of his door making a resounding echo in the quiet hills.

The young woman raised her hand in greeting and then continued trying to loosen the impacable bolts. The farmer ambled slowly toward her, his sharp eyes taking in every detail of the picture she made. Wavy chestnut hair pulled tightly behind her ears into a knot at the back of her head, giving the effect of barely controlled chaos. Her skin was smooth ivory, flawless but too pale, and perched high on her nose were large tortoiseshell glasses with tinted lenses that hid her eyes from view. As she gave up and stood to wait for him, he noticed that her slender body was almost hidden by a navy-blue blazer and unfashionably long skirt that gave the appearance of being hand-me-downs, although they were obviously new and in good condition.

The farmer stopped for a moment as a wave of nostalgia washed over him. There was something about the woman that reminded him of his wife. He scratched his head thoughtfully. Martha had been the belle of the county. She had been sought by all the young bucks and fought over by many. In her day she had been a great beauty. If this woman qualified as a head-turner, she hid it well. Still there was an essence about her, an aura that suggested untapped possibilities.

He shrugged his shoulders and started forward to see what he could do with the tire. Martha had been dead now for close to a decade. He must be getting old, seeing shadows of the past where there were no shadows to be seen.

Lesley Janet Belmont waved goodbye as the pickup rumbled over the hill. With an uncharacteristic display of annoyance, she kicked the spare tire that was now firmly at home on the rear wheel of her Pinto. She was late. Very late. As if this interview wasn't going to be difficult enough!

"I hope this Travis Hagen is a patient man," she grunted as the car started up with a reassuring purr. Considering everything that had gone wrong that morning, she would not have been surprised to have something happen to the engine as well as the tire. It had just been that kind of day.

Count the good things, she admonished herself. At least she hadn't broken down very far from her destination and help had been available when she needed it. Digging deeper

for Pollyannaisms, she drew a blank; nothing else positive could be said for that nauseatingly sunny April
morning.

First, she had awakened late because the station her
clock radio was tuned to was playing soft lilting Strauss
waltzes, and they had woven themselves into her dreams
instead of pulling her out of them. Then the frozen waffle
she'd pulled from the freezer as an emergency breakfast
had remained slightly frozen as she gulped it down, too
rushed to put it through the toaster a second time.

But the worst thing about the morning had been knowing that she, who specialized in interacting only with microfilm and dusty tomes, was going to be forced to spend
this lovely spring day interviewing southwestern Virginia's most famous playboy. "My biorhythms have com-
petely lost the beat," she muttered.

Even though Lesley was late for the appointment that
her boss had arranged for her, she found that she lacked
the courage to speed on the twisting blacktop, and she
gripped the steering wheel tightly in exasperation. According to her calculations she had less than a mile to go.
As she was concentrating so hard on the driveways and
occasional mailboxes lining the road, the neat farms
rimmed with stands of red bud trees and white dogwood
failed to catch her attention. Usually an ardent fan of
Mother Nature's springtime palette she was oblivious to
the scenery.

A lock of hair escaped the knot at the back of her head.
The severe hair style was an everyday solution to the
problem of her unruly hair. Today, knowing that she had
to conduct this interview, she had attempted to make it
tighter than usual—and as a result, her head had begun to
ache in protest. Refusing to be daunted, Lesley pushed the
stray lock behind her ear and continued her search for the
correct driveway.

"It just makes sense. His house is impossible to find." Travis Hagen couldn't have chosen to live in one of the little towns in the area with street names and reassuring numbers. No, he had chosen to live in the midst of this splendid but frustrating-to-navigate scenery. And now on top of everything else that had gone wrong that day, she realized that she had in all probability passed her destination.

Lesley pulled the little car to the side of the road, this time to consult the copy of the hand-drawn map at her side. Printed on cream-colored stationery with royal-blue ink, a child might have thought that the map was a masterpiece of comic ingenuity. Little impish creatures were sprinkled over the labyrinth of winding lines representing roads in the county. Balloons over their heads gave helpful hints such as "Turn that car; you've gone too far."

Her fingers itching to tear the paper into tiny shreds, Lesley jerked the steering wheel and headed back up the road she had just traveled, making a sharp right onto a gravel drive and heading down into what appeared to be nothing but woods. "Don't give up the fight; there's a house in sight," read the caption placed on the map in the vicinity of the driveway Lesley was attempting to maneuver.

The woods lining the road were blazing with color, and Lesley drove so slowly that she couldn't fail to notice them. The dogwood bloomed merrily, along with the white confederate violets she loved, and here and there she saw snatches of flame azalea. Hands gripping the wheel and foot heavy on the brake, she continued her slow descent. The clearing, when she reached it, was a surprise.

The house she had been seeking was nestled on the side of the mountain among the trees, like a queen surrounded by loyal subjects. The view was breathtaking. Although the mountain certainly was not deserted, not another house could be seen anywhere from the site.

The structure was constructed of native stone and giant hand-hewn logs. There were windows visible everywhere and a series of decks that wrapped around the house at different levels to catch the variety of views. Several out-buildings built from weathered barn boards were set at a distance from the house. The intriguing mixture of country charm and contemporary chic captivated Lesley. What did this house have to do with a man who drew silly maps and wrote one of the most beloved comic strips in America? She sighed, wishing she didn't have to find out. The exterior calm that she usually hid behind so well had been shaken by the events of the morning.

The inevitable had been put off long enough. Opening the door and swinging her long legs around, Lesley stepped unwillingly out of the car. As always the clear, clean mountain air was a pleasant shock. The hours she spent at her desk never adequately prepared her for the freshness of the outdoors. She took a deep breath and exhaled slowly. Then, for good measure, she repeated the procedure.

Climbing the short path to the house, she continued to admire the architecture. The thought that something vital was missing nagged at her and it took her a moment to figure out what it was. Instead of the landscaping she would have expected to find in a house of this magnitude there was nothing. Her eyes searched the grounds questioning the absence of shrubs and flower beds. There were giant maple and tulip poplar trees but nothing else was planted close to the house. It was almost as if after building this magnificent structure, someone had lost his enthusiasm.

The sound of the door opening chased all thoughts of landscaping out of Lesley's head. Leaning against the doorframe, holding a plate and munching on a sandwich, was a man so interesting to look at that for a moment she entirely forgot to be shy. Some things are improved by their capture on film, but none of the pictures she had seen could possibly have done justice to this man.

In his early thirties and more than six feet tall, Travis Hagen had a large rangy frame that she would have expected to find on a baseball player or a cowboy. A deep tan set off the surprisingly blue eyes, and the light brown, sunstreaked hair that fell onto his forehead just missed covering them. He was dressed in crisp blue jeans and a red V-neck pullover shirt set off by a gold chain with a medallion nestled in the curly hair visible on his tanned chest. His face lit up with a broad grin as he pushed his shoulder away from the doorframe. Transferring his sandwich to the plate, he wiped his right hand casually on his pants in seeming anticipation of a handshake.

Lesley groaned inwardly, infused by shyness and a return of the reticence she had experienced while driving to the house. He was apparently amused to see her. Hadn't Gerald said the interview was all arranged? She flogged herself with a mental cat-o'-nine-tails for not calling first. Hesitating, she finally extended her hand.

"Hello, Mr. Hagen. I'm Lesley Belmont from the Christiansburg College Department of Mass Communications." She was jolted out of her embarrassment by the warmth of the big hand holding hers.

"Well, Miss Belmont, you're quite a surprise." Travis Hagen's eyes burned a slow trail down from her glasses to her well shaped but clumsily covered body. "Quite a surprise."

Lesley tried to pull back her hand but found it was being held quite firmly. She met his eyes with a trace of nervousness. "I think you have something there that belongs to me, Mr. Hagen."

The grin seemed to broaden imperceptibly but enough to show even, white teeth and a firm, strong jawline. He gave her hand a warm squeeze before he took the right hand he was holding and placed it in her left hand, covering them both for a moment with his own. The sensation he created sent an electrical charge coursing through her body. Following close behind was a desire to put this good-looking and much-too-aware-of-it man in his place. But snappy comebacks were not her forte, and she contented herself with trying to return the stare that she perceived as insolent at best.

"I hope you were expecting me, Mr. Hagen," she continued, tilting her chin in an unconscious effort to appear in control. "Dr. Putfark insisted that I didn't need to call you to confirm our interview."

"Believe me, I know just how insistent your Dr. Putfark can be." His voice was huskily resonant and deep, just what she would have expected to coordinate with his masculine good looks.

"Well, I'm sorry I'm so late."

"I'll bet you're going to tell me that you got lost. T.J.'s map leaves a bit to be desired unless you're familiar with this hill country." He turned to one side motioning her through the door. Because he didn't move far enough out of the way to avoid her entrance completely, Lesley brushed against him lightly, annoyed at the flustered feeling that touching him created.

"I had a flat tire. And yes, your map was a bit...inadequate." She looked around in awe at the room she was entering. Wood, glass, stone and views of some of the prettiest countryside ever merged to create a harmonious picture.

"Not my map. T.J.'s, my son. He drew the original last year for a fifth grade geography class project. The little cartoon characters are his touch of whimsy." There was a hint of pride in his voice.

Lesley felt a surge of relief. This man was married. This man was married? Before attempting this interview she had ransacked the library, looking for information to familiarize herself with Travis Hagen's work. How could her sources, old though they were, have failed to mention a wife and child? The only personal life that the handsome cartoonist seemed to be renowned for was the succession of beautiful women who climbed in and out of his bed. For once, she was glad that her information was incorrect. If he was not the Don Juan that he appeared to be from the publicity about him, then her job today was simpler and safer.

Travis Hagen watched the progression of expressions flicker across her face; her thoughts were unmistakable even with the big dark glasses that almost hid her eyes. He grinned in amusement. "You're not safe, you know. T.J.'s mother and I are divorced. I live alone."

Lesley turned toward the windows, hiding the pink cheeks that she knew were visibly marking her embarrassment at her own transparency. She examined the room as she struggled to regain the composure that she usually wrapped around her like a cloak of armor. The room was furnished in rugged comfortable chairs and sofas most suitable to a den or family room. The wide oak flooring was partially covered in nondescript throw rugs and there were several abstract paintings on the wall. The paintings were the only personal touches. Positioned carelessly over the mantle of a gigantic fieldstone fireplace, they seemed out of place and forlorn.

Lesley turned again and tried to look casually at the man behind her. "Your home is lovely. I'm sure you never get tired of those views."

"There are some views a man never grows tired of."
Again Lesley felt the power of his eyes examining her.

"Mr. Hagen, I'm here to collect some information
about you for the research project that we're doing. I'd like
to get started as soon as possible so that I won't take up too
much of your valuable time." Fighting to keep her voice
level and under control, she concentrated on not letting
this outrageously attactive man unnerve her.

He held the plate up in front of him, wiggling it from
side to side. "You caught me eating lunch. All you can do
now is agree to have a sandwich with me. I've never been
able to talk sense on an empty stomach."

Lesley shook her head firmly. "Of course, I'll be glad to
wait until you're done, but I don't need a sandwich."

"Don't tell me you're one of these women who doesn't
eat. I make a mean bologna sandwich. With or without
mustard?" His slow grin was infectious and the corners of
her mouth relaxed as if they were almost ready to break
free from her rigid control.

"I never eat bologna. Only salad for lunch. It's health-
ier." Her voice, even to her own ears, sounded self-
righteous. It's time to stop acting like Little Miss Muffet,
she chastised herself. This man wanted a sandwich for
lunch. Not her. Travis Hagen could not have failed to notice that Lesley Belmont was not the material passionate
encounters were made from.

"I'll tell you what, I'll compromise. I'll fix you a bologna sandwich with lettuce and tomato on it and then you
can take the bologna off and throw it in the garbage when
I'm not looking." He turned and headed out of the room,
giving Lesley no choice except to follow him.

The kitchen when they reached it was a gourmet's delight with understated efficiency and every possible modern appliance. Copper pots and pans in need of polishing,
accompanied by a collection of utensils to use with them,

hung from big hand-hewn beams. Lesley noticed that they were all covered with a thin layer of dust. If bologna sandwiches were the specialty of the house, she could understand why. She found a stool and sat uneasily on it while she watched the large man stoop to retrieve something from the refrigerator and then stand, almost banging his head on a hanging frying pan.

"Someday I'm going to give all this paraphernalia to Goodwill." He gestured at the collection of pans and utensils. "T.J.'s mother appointed herself to furnishing the kitchen after I had the house built. My idea of furnishing a kitchen is to put in a sink, stove and refrigerator. Then buy a few pans and pots, a spatula and a can opener." He stopped and looked at Lesley. "Right?"

"Don't forget the lettuce crisper, the salad spinner, the parmesan grater..." she answered mildly.

"Women." He slapped two pieces of white bread together with mustard and bologna. "I lied about the lettuce and tomato. I try to prohibit vegetables from using my refrigerator."

Lesley reached tentatively for the sandwich, carefully avoiding his fingers. Without meaning to, she found herself trying to remember if she had ever touched a man who was so attractive before. The unwelcome thought filled her with fleeting disgust.

"I'll bet you drink milk or herb tea with your lunch, right?" Travis Hagen had his back to her, digging in the refrigerator again. "All I have, I'm afraid, is Coke or root beer. You look like the root beer type."

"I guess I'm supposed to ask what the root-beer type is." In spite of herself, Lesley found that she was beginning to relax. Wariness was slipping away and she found his banter easy to respond to.

"Someone who has to convince herself that there is something redeeming in every small lapse of virtue. I've seen people swig down gallons of this stuff because they've heard that it comes from sassafras root, or did originally...and call me Travis, please."

"I'll have a Coke, Travis." She smiled at him, wondering if perhaps she had completely blown out of proportion the information that she had read on this man. Travis Hagen seemed like a nice enough human being. Certainly he was taking her presence there with good grace. The warm gaze and the playful innuendos were probably the natural by-products of being such a gorgeous member of the species: homo sapiens hunkus incredilibus.

Lesley took the time to examine Travis closely as he poured her Coke, oblivious to her scrutiny. His natural virility was accented by heavy-lidded blue eyes and a lithe muscular body. The boyish grin and the thick fringe of hair falling onto his forehead served only to accent his completely masculine presence. It was a combination that women invariably found irresistible. She was sure that he could take his pick from the female masses.

It was time to remember why she was there. "Until I started this part of our research project, I thought that everyone who did comic strips lived in New York City. I was really surprised to find out from your syndicate that you lived so close to Christiansburg." She took the Coke he offered and sipped it, watching him over the rim of the glass as he pulled his stool up to the counter by her side.

"That's one of the advantages of my profession. When it came time for me to take over the strip from my father, I was able to settle almost anywhere I wanted. I'm much more at home here in the mountains than I ever would be in New York."

"But you were from New York originally, weren't you?"

"You've been doing some homework, I see."

Lesley was warming to the subject, forgetting to be self-conscious. "Lots of it. I found some articles about the history of your strip, and they gave some good background about how your grandfather started it and your father took over. Unfortunately, the articles were old so I didn't get much information on your contributions. And the more recent articles I saw on you weren't very informative about your comic strip."

"I don't like to give interviews. Invariably reporters concentrate on my other more personal talents, not my artistic ones." He grinned at her embarrassed wince.

"But I do know that when your father did 'The Family Jones,' he lived in New York," she continued, trying not to acknowledge the grin.

He nodded. "I always thought it was a bit strange to have a comic strip about a rural farming family written in the biggest city in America. These mountains seem like home to me and to the Jones family too."

"Well, it was a real gift to the project to have you so close by. Gerald would have had to run up quite a phone bill interviewing you in New York."

"Gerald?"

"Dr. Putfark," she amended.

"Don't you usually do the interviewing for him?"

"Actually, no," she said, shaking her head. "In fact, I hardly get out of the library most of the time. But Gerald asked me to come today."

"And why was that?" Travis asked with another grin.

It was a question she had asked herself when Gerald had called her late one night earlier in the week and demanded that she do this interview. "I'm not sure," Lesley answered vaguely. "He said I'd be perfect for the job." They finished their sandwiches in silence.

"Tell me about yourself, Lesley. How did you get a job reading comic strips?" He wiped his hands and turned, his face too close for her to feel comfortable.

She sat back distancing herself slightly, picking up her glass as an excuse. "That's not all there is to this, I assure you. We're examining various media that make reference to family life. Then we analyze them to see what they are saying about the way American families live." Lesley felt her fingers making warm, slippery paths down the icy glass and she set it carefully on the counter. "Comic strips are big business, along with television, movies and popular novels. What you are saying about and to Americans everywhere is important."

Travis smiled slightly at her serious face. "I had no idea that 'The Family Jones' would be considered social commentary by anyone. I make it a point to stay away from politics and religion."

"We both know that's not true. I've been able to see enough of your strips to know that they're rife with political comment. They're just very subtle. The message is even more far-reaching that way, I'll bet." She shook her head slightly as he smiled at her. "But it's not really the politics we're after anyhow. It's the way your characters interact, what they worry about, how they feel, who they are that's important for this project."

"This Futspack character said that mine was only one of about two dozen strips that you're going to study. How many other cartoonists are going to receive a personal visit?" He moved slightly closer, offsetting the distance that she had put between them.

"Dr. Putfark, you mean? We're only going to do personal interviews with about a half-dozen cartoonists. You were chosen because your strip is unique. It's one of the few that's had characters who age with it. But most of the research is straightforward content analysis. All we need are copies of the strips." Lesley could no longer ignore the ever-narrowing distance between them nor the calculating gleam in his eyes. Her wariness returned with the force of an explosion.

"You know, Lesley, I was surprised to find out just how...important...this kind of research could be." Travis pushed his plate back and propped his elbow on the table, moving even closer to her in the process. "Take this project, for instance. It must be very important. I gathered from Dr. Bisfork that it was practically vital to the security of American families everywhere, so vital in fact that he would do almost anything to get his information. Almost anything."

Lesley felt a cold shiver go up her spine. She folded her arms across her chest in an automatic attempt to protect herself as she tried to respond to his comment seriously. "Of course, we don't feel it's *that* important, but when you put a lot of yourself into something you want to be sure it turns out well."

Travis smiled, his eyes closing slightly. "Mmm...and have you put a lot of yourself into it, Lesley?"

"I work very hard, Mr. Hagen."

"Travis."

"Strange," Lesley murmured. "A few minutes ago calling you Travis seemed like a good idea."

Travis rose and leisurely began to clear off the counter. "Dr. Futzpark seemed to want this interview very badly," he said. "Do you know how badly he wanted it?"

Lesley's stomach dropped to her toes. With a lifetime of practice, she had gotten very good at interpreting innuendos. There were enough innuendos here to keep her busy for a decade. "I'm sure that he was persuasive. Your cooperation was vital for the research to be as good as we hope it will be. But I'm sorry if he was too pushy. His dedication can get a bit overwhelming at times."

"Dedication...that's an interesting choice of words. It implies all sorts of promises made, commitments that need to be kept." His sexy, lopsided smile had disappeared to be replaced by what Lesley tried not to identify as a leer. "Tell me, are you anywhere near as dedicated as Tuffkarp is?"

She sat up straighter, her spine stiffening. "I take this research very seriously. I hope that's what you're asking, Mr. Hagen."

"No, it's not entirely what I'm asking, Lesley. Sometimes people are so dedicated that they'll do all sorts of things to meet their goals." He stopped in front of her and lightly rested his hand on her shoulder. The subtle pressure seemed to burn a hole through the thin cotton material of the blouse and jacket. "Has anyone ever told you that you have beautiful skin?" he asked, as a fingertip came up to caress her cheek with a whisper-soft touch before descending to her shoulder once again to hold her firmly in place.

"Not in the last twenty-six years," she choked.

"I can't see how they failed to mention it. You must have other attributes that distracted them." There was no question about it, the expression on Travis's face was a leer. And he was examining her with more than professional interest.

"I have a tremendously high IQ and I won fourth place in the broad jump my second year at Clifton Junior High," Lesley babbled. "I've been knocking people dead for years with those attributes."

He dismissed her comments with a shake of his head as his fingers began to knead her shoulders. "Those lovely long legs should have taken first place easily."

"I was knock-kneed and pigeon-toed. I wore saddle oxfords until I was fourteen."

"Your orthopedist should be proud."

Lesley stood, pushing the stool with her legs to begin backing away from Travis. "My orthopedist, my orthodontist, my plastic surgeon..."

"Plastic surgeon?"

Actually that part was an exaggeration. When she was fifteen a bad case of poison ivy had sent her to see a dermatologist who also dabbled in plastic surgery. In the small town Lesley had grown up in, no doctor could afford only one specialty. "I'm really a very ordinary person," she said, shrugging her shoulders in the hope that Travis would notice his hands were still firmly weighting them down.

"Somehow I think we're on different wavelengths," he said, dropping his hands to his side. While he hesitated as if to decide on his next move, Lesley took the opportunity to back farther away.

"Mr. Hagen. This research is very important and we are willing to accommodate you to do it. That's why I drove all the way over here from Christiansburg to meet with you. I'm sure your time is very precious, as is my own, so we ought to get going, don't you think?" She tried to smile reassuringly, but one side of her mouth refused to cooperate.

"Accommodate. Now that's a word I could get to like. Accommodate. I think it usually means bending your desires to meet someone else's, doesn't it?"

Lesley decided that the smile he was giving her was just like the one the wolf had given Little Red Riding Hood before he began to chase her around Granny's bed. "There are limits, of course, to how accommodating I can be." She dodged the hand that seemed about to perch on her shoulder again. The hard counter pressed against her back and she moved carefully to the side until she was free of its restraints.

"Limits. Funny, that's not a word that was in Parkfoot's vocabulary."

What on earth did the man mean? "Well, we're done with lunch now," she managed to say, her voice betraying her confusion. "Are you ready for the interview?"

"Interview? Oh, yes, the interview. Well, to be perfectly honest, that seems to be a dull way to spend such a lovely afternoon, don't you think?" Travis began to stalk her with the agile control of a cat stalking a wounded bird. Lesley imagined that he was mentally licking his lips.

"Mr. Hagen." She felt an urge to turn and run. "I am here to interview you, not for any other reason."

He stopped and looked at her appraisingly, his blue eyes heavy-lidded and mysterious. "Oh, is that what Dr. Fuzzcork told you? I could almost believe that you think that's true."

"Putfark, the man's name is Putfark, P...U...T...F...ARK...Putfark!" She put her hands in front of her, palms out as if to ward off an attacker. The situation was suddenly very clear to her. This man, for some reason that she couldn't fathom, had plans for her afternoon that did not include an academic interview. Totally unequipped to deal with this turn of events, she could only think of one alternative. Retreat. She could think of nothing else to do to salvage the situation.

"I am not here to play silly games with you. We certainly need this research, but I don't need your adolescent antics to brighten up my day." Lesley sidestepped to the counter, and picked up her handbag. Backing slowly out of the kitchen door, she turned and walked quickly through the house trying to remember the way she had come.

The house was imposing inside as well as out, and in her confusion she found herself unsure which way to go to make a hasty exit. Turning in the hall she found to her chagrin that she had made a wrong decision. In front of her was a huge bedroom, complete with a king-sized water bed and a rustic fieldstone fireplace. Footsteps behind her blocked off her intended escape.

"I definitely got up on the wrong side of the bed today," she groaned.

"Perhaps you need to try again." Travis put his hands on her shoulders and turned her around slowly, his fingers attempting to massage the tautness from her body. With disconcerted fascination she watched as he bent, placing his lips firmly against hers. For a split second, before thought intruded, she stood perfectly still, rooted to the spot by the shock of the careless intimacy. Then thought returned.

"Take your hands off me!" Lesley's voice trembled, but she realized that she wasn't frightened. Beneath the anger that was fighting its way to the surface was a deep well of vulnerability and hurt pride. Obviously there was more to this than she understood right now; she was convinced that it was simply not possible that Travis Hagen would find her so appealing that he would make a pass at her at their first meeting. And try as she might, this situation could not be blamed on faulty biorhythms.

Travis watched the expressions crossing Lesley's face. He lifted his right hand and carefully removed the tinted glasses she was wearing. Without them her big golden-brown eyes were clearly visible and he saw the hurt there. She wrenched free of the hand still on her shoulder, not taking time to notice the subtle change in his features.

"You've had your fun," she said as calmly as she could. "I'm leaving now. We can manage without your interview, I'm sure." A need to release some of her anger consumed her. "Do you think that you're so completely irresistible that I would fall salivating at your feet? Did you think you could throw me on that mound of quivering Jell-O in front of the fireplace for a quick tumble before dinner?" She gestured angrily toward the water bed.

"Wait," he said, his voice serious.

"I know I'm not your usual type, Mr. Hagen, but that doesn't mean I don't have feelings. Frankly I'm surprised that a blatant attempt to humiliate me would come from the man who draws such a warm and sensitive portrayal of family life." She caught her breath and lifted her eyes to his. The expression there confused her.

"Damn Putfark," he swore.

"It won't help to blame anyone else for your own arrogance, Mr. Hagen."

"Lesley, I had no idea..."

"Spare me your explanations." She brushed past him, not caring about anything except finding the front door. This time she made the correct turn in the hall and followed it to the entrance. She let herself out with a bang.

Revving the engine on the Pinto she turned in the gravel circle at the end of his driveway and began her ascent up the side of the mountain. Anger and humiliation still consumed her and only when the bright light of early afternoon glared on the unshed tears in her eyes did Lesley realize that her glasses were probably still in Travis Hagen's hand.

## Chapter Two

Hot, soapy water cascaded down Lesley's naked back as she washed her hair for the second time. The pulsating force of the shower and the hard scrubbing she gave her scalp served to help dissolve the tension headache that the long trip home had not dissipated. Hungry for an explanation of the afternoon's events, she had driven directly to the college after leaving Travis Hagen's house, only to find that Gerald had left for the day. As a temporary solution to her turbulent feelings she had stopped and walked through the woods on a trail close to her apartment. The quiet forest had helped her to achieve a measure of calm.

What kind of man would play such spiteful games with her, she wondered as she stood under the pounding beat of the water, letting it rinse the shampoo from her hair until it squeaked. Actually, what kind of men? Gerald had sent her there and Travis had humiliated her. What on earth had she done wrong? How could the situation have gotten so badly out of hand? She had only wanted to do her job.

The persistent ringing of a telephone interrupted her thoughts. Let it ring, she decided. She turned off the shower and grabbed a fluffy bath towel. Still the phone continued to echo through the rooms of the apartment. With a sigh she hastily pulled a pair of faded blue jeans and a thin white T-shirt over her naked, dripping body. Dropping the towel she opened the door and raced for the phone. If it was Gerald, she had plenty to say to him, but she preferred to tackle him in person. On the other hand, the phone call might be her mother. A stab of fear shot through Lesley at the thought that something might have happened to her father. Mr. Belmont had been the recent victim of a mild heart attack, and Lesley's concern for him was always present.

"Mom. I'm glad you called. How's dad doing?"

Her mother's voice sounded far away. "He's doing just fine, honey. We haven't heard from you for a while, so we thought we'd call to see what's going on. We wondered if you'd had any more dates with your new boss yet."

Lesley shook her head in exasperation at the reference to Gerald. Gerald Putfark was her employer. Nothing more. But as usual her family was grasping at straws convinced that she would only be happy when she settled down in wedded bliss. She had made the mistake of going out to dinner with Gerald once, and the even worse mistake of mentioning that date to her mother.

The "we" in her mother's probing obviously referred to her mother and her sister, Jennifer, not her mother and father. Her father was a very private person in a family of avid gossips. His only ally in a houseful of talkative women had been Lesley. She smiled in good-natured acceptance of this fault in her mother's character. Mary Jane Belmont was everything a mother was supposed to be, but with a vengeance.

"How are Jennifer, David and the kids?" Lesley asked, ignoring her mother's question. Idly she reached for a wide-toothed comb to begin teasing the snarls out of her long brown hair. It was a difficult job at best. She listened as her mother talked nonstop about the antics of Jennifer's children.

Lesley continued to inquire about the rest of the family, neatly sidestepping any questions about herself. The apartment was cool and her thick dripping hair had soaked the T-shirt through. She shivered as she looked for something to wrap herself in, regretting that she had dropped her towel in the rush for the phone. Resigning herself to the chill when nothing appeared to be in reach, she listened to her mother chatter on. The sudden squawk of the doorbell snapped Lesley's mind out of automatic pilot. Without bothering to interrupt the flow of her mother's conversation, she covered the receiver. "Who's there?" she called.

"The U.P.S. man."

"Come in," Lesley invited, switching her attention back to the phone conversation. She concentrated on trying to break into her mother's monologue long enough to excuse herself for a moment. When no possibility presented itself she looked up with a humorously pleasing expression to see Travis Hagen standing in her living room.

Leaning casually against the floor-to-ceiling divider separating her living and dining areas, he was obviously enjoying his view of her. With dawning horror, she looked down to see the revealing transparency of her T-shirt and the clinging, snugly fitting jeans.

"Get out!" she mouthed silently, pointing to the door until she realized that the motion pulled the damp shirt even tighter across her breasts. Travis looked at her and shrugged, cupping his hand behind his ear.

Lesley put her hand over the receiver again. "Get out," she said in low tones. "Get out now."

He shook his head with irritating laziness. "No," he mouthed. The exaggerated pantomime looked like a kiss. Lesley stamped her foot and managed to point toward the door with her arm tucked firmly against the revealing shirt. He shook his head again and gestured helplessly.

Turning her back to Travis, Lesley tapped her foot impatiently. After another anecdote, Mrs. Belmont gave her daughter a few last words of motherly advice and the conversation ended. Lesley slammed down the receiver in frustration and turned to face Travis with her arms crossed in front of her, imitating a disgruntled school marm.

"Now those clothes really do something for you." Travis was still leaning comfortably on the divider watching her.

"I want you out of here right now, Travis Hagen! I've seen enough of you to last a lifetime." Lesley pointed to the door, one arm still crossed in front for protection.

"I want to talk to you, Lesley. And I came to return these." He held out the glasses she had left behind.

"You could have sent them through the mail. I see fine without them; it wasn't an emergency." She reached for the glasses but he continued to hold them carefully in his hand.

"I thought the U.P.S. man should deliver them." He smiled wryly. "Don't make me blackmail you with their return. I want to talk to you. Just talk. Please?" He smiled with the genuineness of a little boy caught with his hand in the cookie jar.

Gauging her chances of pushing him out the door without a bulldozer, Lesley relented and nodded stiffly. He stepped closer and handed her the glasses. "Tell me, if you can see fine without them, why do you wear them? They hide some of the prettiest eyes I've ever seen."

Ignoring the compliment she turned and placed the glasses on a table by the phone. Without offering Travis a chair she folded her arms in front of her again and faced him, standing a safe distance away. "What is it that you feel you have to say to me, Mr. Hagen?" An involuntary shiver rippled through her, and Lesley realized that she was still wet and very cold.

Travis noticed the shiver. "You look cold. Doesn't this place have any heat?" He walked to the radiators, placing his hands on them to check their output. Kneeling, he began to fumble with the knobs at the bottom to turn them on.

"Don't do that!" Lesley walked over to the radiator and gestured at the rows of plants sitting on a shelf over the heating unit. "The heat will kill the plants." She stopped when she realized how close she had come to him and began to back away.

"How do you manage in the winter then," he asked curiously as he straightened up to face her. "They can't take freezing temperatures, I'm sure, and neither can you."

"I only move them in here in April. There's a greenhouse that keeps them for me in the winter when the apartment can't offer any sun." She shook her head, trying to get the conversation back on the track. "What do you want to say to me? I'm tired, wet, cold and hungry. Please make this fast."

"For God's sake woman, go put on a sweater. It can wait that long at least."

Lesley shook her head firmly, but as his eyes dropped to the visible outline of her breasts, she fled into her bedroom, grabbing and pulling on a bulky white pullover. She waited a moment to compose herself before reentering the living room.

Travis was wandering around the small room, looking at the decorations on the wall. "These creatures are wonderful." He looked at Lesley and pointed at a soft sculpture hanging from silky cords. "I like this one especially.

But I have to admit that I don't know what it is." He angled his head and stepped backward regarding the animal carefully. "I'd say it was a cross between a lizard and a dragon. Am I right?"

Lesley waited silently for him to get to the purpose of his visit.

"You made them, didn't you?" he prodded.

She nodded stiffly.

"This one here," Travis said as he walked to another creature suspended from the ceiling on a fine nylon thread, "this is impressive. It's a butterfly about to take flight, isn't it?"

"Yes."

Lesley watched him warily as he continued to examine her apartment. She was puzzled by what was obviously his genuine interest. Looking around she tried to see the room through his eyes. The soft browns and beiges of the overstuffed furniture were highlighted by accents of bright golds, hot pinks and brilliant blues. She had filled the apartment with healthy ferns and decorated with her own abstract needlepoint pillows. The most unusual decorations, however, were the soft sculpture insects that she had created. Begun as whimsical gifts for Jennifer's oldest daughter, the collection had grown and Lesley had found that they provided an outlet for a side of her that was not expressed anywhere else. Watching Travis Hagen examine her creations was a little like letting him into her soul. She didn't like it.

"Mr. Hagen. I think I mentioned that I was tired and hungry, as well as cold. If you don't mind, I'd like to get this over with."

Travis looked at his watch. "It is dinnertime. Can I take you out to eat? We could have our discussion over a nice thick steak somewhere." He watched as Lesley shook her head firmly. "Let me order a pizza then; we can talk over pepperoni and mushrooms." He cocked his eyebrows as she shook her head still another time. "If you have some bologna, I make a mean bologna sandwich."

Lesley shrugged in exasperation. "Please get to the point."

"I can't talk on an empty stomach." Travis smiled disarmingly.

She let out a groan of frustration. "All right. I'll make you a salad if it will get you out of here quicker." She turned and entered the kitchen, aware that he was following.

"I usually only eat meat for dinner, never salad." He was standing behind her and, hating herself for it, she felt again the physical attraction that she had been aware of earlier in the day.

"I'll tell you what, then. I'll make you a lettuce and to- mato sandwich with bologna on it. Then you can..."

"I can throw the lettuce and tomato away when you're not looking." He chuckled softly. "I'll bet you've never let a piece of bologna into this kitchen ever."

Lesley opened the refrigerator to take out the salad in- gredients. "You know, Mr. Hagen. I have this theory. There are two kinds of people. Those who eat bologna and those who don't. You might say that the first kind are..."

"Full of bologna?"

"Exactly."

"I'm sure I deserved that." His voice was sincere.

Lesley looked at him in surprise. The small kitchen seemed dominated by his presence. He was leaning against the sink, his thumbs hooked in the pockets of his blue jeans, and his hair had fallen over his forehead as it seemed to have a habit of doing. She forgot to feel angry as a twinge of curiosity overtook her. "I'd love to have you elaborate on that."

Travis reached for the medallion around his neck, idly pulling it back and forth on the chain. "I'm not good at apologies, since I rarely do anything wrong, so this will probably take some doing to get it right." He flashed a quick smile.

"God save me from conceited men." Lesley turned her attention to the salad, waiting for him to go on.

"I'll start at the beginning."

"Sensible."

"This Professor Mudpack fellow called me about a month ago and wanted to arrange an interview. He was arrogant and demanding. I told him that I'd be happy to help when my schedule permitted, but that for the next month I was probably going to be too busy developing a new story line for the strip; I asked him to get back to me in a month or so." Travis stopped playing with the medallion and jammed his hands back in his pockets.

"Go on."

"He kept calling anyway, getting more and more demanding and pushy. He even called me late at night sometimes. I finally told him that as far as I was concerned he could take his research and, well...put it somewhere."

Lesley smiled faintly, wondering how this piece of homespun advice had sounded to Gerald.

"Instead of taking my gentle hint, he kept calling, only this time he tried offering me incentives." Travis ran his hands through the hair on his forehead, managing to push it out of his eyes for a moment before it fell across them again.

"What kind of incentives?" Lesley's mind was whirling, anticipating what she was about to hear.

"Well, at first the good professor just mentioned things like added prestige, publicity about 'The Family Jones' when the research was published. That kind of thing. I guess it got to be a game of cat and mouse. I was direct with him at first, but he kept coming back with different angles. Eventually I found myself falling into the spirit of the whole thing. I used to be quite a talented practical joker and I suppose I haven't completely outgrown the tendency. Anyway, I found Dudmark to be so self-righteous and obnoxious that I let my better judgment lapse, I guess.''

"I guess." Lesley's voice was noncommital but she felt a flash of the hurt that she had experienced earlier in the day. "Go on."

"My schedule finally cleared up a bit. I decided to take a few days off and forget about the strip. I figured that way I might be able to come up with a new story line." Travis turned his head slowly, no longer looking at her. "Bismark called me that day with a new suggestion."

"Putfark."

"Yes, Putfark. He suggested that if I didn't want him to do the interview, maybe I'd let someone else do it. I told him only if she was five-foot-five, remarkably good-looking and a wonder in bed."

There was a pregnant silence. Lesley stoically waited for the rest of the story.

"Of course I wasn't serious and Putfark knew it. I thought that would be the end of it. I was thoroughly disenchanted with the idea of participating in this research. My intention was to let him know in no uncertain terms that I didn't want anything to do with it. My next step was going to be to get an unlisted telephone number."

"It's too bad you didn't think of that before."

"The next day, Butquirk called back and said that he was going to take me up on my condition. He was sending his five-foot-five gorgeous research assistant out to get the information from me."

"And then I showed up." Lesley's voice caught slightly. "And you thought that you'd teach Gerald a thing or two by humiliating me."

"I thought you were part of the game. I was sure that even this Gruntbark character wouldn't send you into this situation without enlightening you. So I assumed that you were playing along with the joke when you arrived."

"Well, I guess you got the shock of your life; I know I did." Lesley began to toss the salad. What a surprise she must have given Travis when she showed up at his door. Five-foot-eight and definitely not what he'd expected. "Tell me, do you make a habit of making passes at unsuspecting strangers? Or a habit of letting strange men set you up with women as bribes?"

Travis was silent and Lesley finished tossing the salad. Finding nothing else to do, she brushed past him, carrying the bowl into the dining area and setting it down on the lovely antique oak dining table. Travis followed her at a safe distance. She got plates and silverware out of a small china cabinet and set the table hurriedly. She was in no mood to drag out the evening.

Halfway through the salad, Travis set down his fork. "I don't think I've explained myself very well. I reacted like a little kid to Putfark, I guess. He was such a pompous ass, I finally decided to put him in his place. But I never intended to hurt you. I thought you were playing along. I had no intention of following through on Putfark's bribe and I'm sure he knew that. I just thought I'd play the game a while longer. You were so cute with your solemn attitude and your intensity. I've never seen anyone so serious about comic strips before."

Lesley chocked on a slice of tomato and took a sip of ice water. "Cute!"

Travis examined her curiously. "Definitely. Those clothes you were wearing looked like something from an advertisement for the young academic. I was sure you were teasing me."

Lesley shook back her hair bravely. "I assure you, I was not teasing you. I was just dressing for the occasion. Or at least what I thought the occasion was supposed to be: a simple professional interview. I suppose you were expecting a plunging neckline and skirt cut halfway up my thighs."

"Actually that T-shirt you have on under that sweater would have done nicely," he said with a grin.

Standing abruptly Lesley began to clear off the plates, taking Travis's half-eaten salad back into the kitchen. He rose and followed her to the door.

Leaning on one elbow, he watched her move around the kitchen. "I really didn't have any idea that you were bothered by my teasing."

"Teasing," she sputtered. "Teasing? That's what you call it? Try 'making fun of, humiliating, embarrassing.' They all seem to fit better."

"But I never meant to, Lesley." His voice sounded strangely like a caress. "I liked you right away, but I was still angry at Stutgard and I guess a bit at you too for coming at his bidding. I was just making a good-natured pass at you."

"To get even with Gerald?"

"Mostly because I thought you were an attractive young woman. I didn't think you'd find it so upsetting." He laughed softly. "I've had women turn me down before, but never has anyone seemed so completely humiliated by my attentions. And really, I didn't realize until I saw your eyes that I'd hurt you. I'm not sure I understand why you were so upset, but I'm truly sorry for being so insensitive."

Lesley stopped and stared at Travis. He was watching her, a sincere look of concern in his eyes. She realized that he was telling her the truth; he had not been making fun of her. And he *had* found her cute or interesting or attractive in some way. The thought so astounded her that she lost all ability to answer him. She just stared helplessly.

"You're supposed to tell me that you understand and that I'm forgiven," he prompted her.

She nodded, still staring.

The corners of his mouth turned up lazily. "Then I'm off the hook. Now will you let me finish my salad or feed me something solid?"

She smiled tentatively in answer, reaching in the refrigerator for cheese and bread. "Finish the salad and I'll make you a grilled cheese." He reached for his plate and ate his salad in the doorway watching her cook. She reminded herself that it wasn't safe to trust him, even though he had apologized, but now she at least didn't mind having him there.

She made coffee and they carried the sandwich and cups into the living room. Travis lounged in his chair, tipping it back on its hind legs. "You know, I'd really be glad to help with your research. Sort of a concrete apology. If you still want to interview me I'll be available to you, but never to Harold Putfutz."

Lesley smiled inwardly at the new addition to the series of purposely inaccurate names. "I'm much too tired tonight to think about the interview. But I'd like to do it soon. I still have to work for Dr. Putfark and it will be easier if I get the interview."

Travis looked at her knowingly. "Oh, I don't think you'll have to worry about the good professor."

She put her cup down with a suspicious thud. "Why not and how would you know?" she said slowly.

"He and I had a little chat today."

"Chat?"

"I called him to get your address. I just happened to tell him what I thought of him at the same time. And I told him that if he gave you one moment's grief over this, I'd see that no one cooperated with his research again."

Lesley suddenly understood why Gerald had been gone when she had arrived at the office. A small tingle of pleasure shot through her. "Do you have that kind of power?"

"Enough to influence the people that count in this case. My syndicate, other cartoonists I know, several major newspapers." Travis looked pleased with himself.

"Just how did Gerald take your ultimatum?" Lesley thought she could make a good guess.

"How does this Bisquick fellow take anything? He was not pleased. I could almost hear the wheels of revenge spinning."

Lesley sat quietly contemplating Travis's words. This latest and most repugnant of Gerald's schemes had wiped away any civil feelings she had harbored for him. She was left with a feeling of regret that an otherwise intelligent human being could be so vindictive and childish. Her career was another problem entirely. She hoped that Travis Hagen had convinced Gerald not to take his anger out on her.

"Travis," she said tentatively, "I would appreciate it if you'd let me set up the interview. After I finish it I'm going to have to spend several weeks at the university and public libraries going through microfilm so I can complete the content analysis on your strip."

"Why microfilm?"

"That's the only way to see back copies of all strips that we're scheduled to analyze."

"That seems like a lot of trouble. I know a much easier way to get hold of them." Travis put down his empty cup, stretched and stood. Lesley admired the pure animal grace of the movement. He moved like a jungle cat, power and grace combined.

"How's that?"

"Use my files. I have copies of every episode of 'The Family Jones' that's ever been done. Three generations of them. Actually, I have pretty complete files on some other strips too. They might save you some time at the library."

"Where do you keep these files?" Lesley stood and followed Travis toward the door.

"At my house, in my office." He smiled down at her as he leaned on the doorframe. "It will mean bearding the lion in his den."

"Can I take that chance?"

"I wouldn't consider touching a woman who didn't want me. If it's to be hands off, then it will be hands off. And I won't tease you either." He gave her a lingering perusal before he opened the door. "But I'll have to admit my hunting instincts have been aroused. I've never met anyone so delightfully shy and perplexed by male attention."

Lesley blushed at the strange compliment, sure that she was cementing his opinion of her as a creature from the nineteenth century. "That's the first time anyone has ever seen my shyness as an asset, but under this trembling exterior beats a steadfast heart. Can I interview you tomorrow?"

"Lunch? Bring lettuce and tomato, I'll supply the..."

"Bologna," they finished together.

"Thank you for dinner, Lesley." Travis was down the stairs two steps at a time and out the front door of the building as she watched. She experienced a feeling of regret at his going. Still wary, she had to concede that he had brought a warmth and vitality with him when he entered the little apartment.

Sitting on the sofa she hugged a stuffed ladybug. So Travis Hagen's attentions had not been a malicious attempt to humiliate her. How much of what had happened earlier had been his fault and how much of it had been her own overwrought interpretation of the events? She realized now that she wasn't blameless. She had allowed herself to be completely unnerved by a fairly innocent flirtation. There had been only playful innuendos and one brief kiss. It had been enough to put a stop to, but not enough to send her running home with her tail between her legs.

Still hugging the ladybug, Lesley got up and turned on a tape of classical music. Certainly she had outgrown some of her adolescent lack of self-esteem, but today was proof that there was still a lot of it present. She had always been unsure of herself around men, hesitating to put herself in the position of being hurt, but her overreaction today was something to contemplate. Lying on the sofa she let the music drift over her as she dug a little deeper.

Having two beautiful sisters, and being sandwiched in between them like a piece of dried-up cheese on freshly baked bread, had been a difficult way to grow up. Lesley had been tall and awkward and they had been short and bouncy. She had been dark like her father and they had been blond like her mother. They had perfect teeth; she had worn braces. The eternally pink dresses that her mother had insisted the three of them wear looked awful on Lesley and wonderful on them. Jennifer had been a cheerleader; Maribeth had excelled in drama; and Lesley had quietly gotten straight A's. Why did I see that as a shortcoming, she wondered.

Jennifer had married right out of high school; Maribeth had moved to New York to break into the theater; and Lesley had gone to Duke University on scholarship. Was that a failure? Would life have been much different for her if she hadn't always had the competition to deal with? She supposed it would have been easier, but she loved her sisters and she couldn't imagine growing up without them

They had been close to her in every way. They had taken her failures personally and tried to mold her in their images. In turn she had helped them pass tests, write papers, and had listened patiently to their agonized outpourings over unhappy love affairs.

Lesley sat up as the tape ended and stretched, the movement bringing back into focus the picture of Travis Hagen. She had seen him as menacing, as a deliberate insult to her fragile feminine ego. Instead he claimed to have seen her as an attractive woman. The thought gave her pause. She rose and went into her bedroom, stripping off the sweater. Walking to the full-length mirror on the back of the door she forced herself to look carefully at what she saw there.

She was tall; that was nothing new. She was thin, but not too thin to discourage the firm swelling breasts or the graceful hips. Examining her face, she was more critical. She was very pale, without the naturally rosy cheeks of Jennifer or Maribeth. Her mop of curling brown hair fell in wild disarray well past her shoulder blades. She pushed it back, revealing the widow's peak that made it so hard to part successfully. There was nothing really wrong with her features, she decided, except that they were not what she had dreamed of having. She had desperately wanted a snub nose like Jennifer's. Instead hers was long and straight. And she had ached for a rosebud mouth like Maribeth's. Instead hers was full, almost sensual.

Sensual? That was a misnomer. Gerald would laugh at that description. Failing to get her into his bed after their only date, he had labeled her lack of interest in him as frigidity. Gerald notwithstanding, Lesley doubted sometimes if she had any sensuality at all. The men she had dated in college had failed to provoke any feelings within her except mild affection.

Undressing, she slipped into a full-length cotton night-
gown that hid all signs of her body. Would Travis Hagen
find her disappointing, she wondered? Deciding that she
was crazy to be thinking that way, she picked up her brush
and pulled it through her long hair, wincing with every one
of the one hundred strokes. Travis had been flirtatious and
he had been kind. But genuine interest? Lesley was sure
that it was absent. By no stretch of her overactive imagination could she pretend that a man like Travis Hagen
would want a woman like Lesley Belmont. She was far
from being the hopeless case that she had considered herself in high school years, but she was equally far from
being one of the ravishing women that Travis Hagen must
have in his life. Still it gave her feminine self-esteem a boost
to realize that Travis had been interested enough to pursue her to her apartment.

Coming back from the bathroom Lesley turned back the
handmade quilt covering her bed and slipped under the
sheets. She cradled her head on her hands and pulled up
her knees like a small child. The stillness of the apartment
was usually pleasant. Growing up in a small house and
sharing a bedroom with two other girls, she had always
longed for a place of her own. Tonight, however, she
wished that she was a child again, sleeping next to Jennifer. Or perhaps it was something else that she really
wanted. She sighed deeply and concentrated on breathing
slowly. She would need a good night's sleep. Tomorrow she
would see Gerald and Travis. And Lesley was sure that
she'd need her wits about her for both confrontations.

# Chapter Three

"Has the king of comic strip interpretation made it in yet, Sylvia?" Lesley leaned against the desk of the reception area of the Christiansburg College building that housed the Department of Mass Communications. A fairly new department, they had been assigned one of the wooden, temporary buildings as their headquarters. It was one of Gerald's pet peeves to have been cast off on the outskirts of the sprawling campus with only one secretary.

"King Gerald got here at the crack of dawn, before me in fact. You're later than usual yourself, honey. I'll bet you were up late entertaining some gorgeous man." Sylvia's smile was expectant. The softly rounded, middle-aged woman was Lesley's friend and a Mary Jane Belmont look-alike. Sometimes Lesley wondered how she had gotten lucky enough to leave home and find a surrogate mother sitting in her office every morning.

Sylvia's chance remark set off flashing memories of Travis Hagen, the man she had entertained the previous night. Sylvia would be dazzled if she heard the story, and Lesley would never hear the end of it. She shook her head. "The last time I entertained a man in my apartment was when I watched *Casablanca* on the late, late show, and Humphrey didn't even stay for the commercials."

"What'z a babe like you doing wastin' your time in a dump like thiz then?" Sylvia quipped in a terrible Bogart imitation.

"Right now, I'm gearing myself up to confront Gerald. Did he ask to see me?"

"No, honey." Sylvia's voice returned to normal. "In fact, if I recollect correctly, he specified that he was not to be disturbed."

"I'll just bet he did." Lesley considered backing down and forgetting about the talk she had planned to have with Gerald. It was a spineless, cowardly thought, but for a moment it was very appealing. "Well," she finally said with a sigh, "I'm going to march right in there and disturb him anyhow."

Sylvia's only answer was to begin humming "Onward Christian Soldiers."

"Come in, come in," the cross voice from the inner sanctum responded to Lesley's knock. Straightening her spine she opened the door. Gerald was sitting in an imitation leather desk chair, his feet propped on the Formica wood-grain desk. He made no move to stand or even sit up when he saw her. "I asked Sylvia not to let anyone disturb me."

"I know you did, Gerald. But as you can see, I'm here anyway." It was not a typical Lesley Belmont approach and Gerald's jaw dropped several inches. Firmly closing the door behind her, Lesley took a seat in front of the desk examining the fading good looks of the man opposite her, who finally sat up in his chair.

Rather short and a bit overweight, Gerald Putfark had probably once been quite a woman pleaser. Now the prominent scowl and the receding hairline highlighted a face not meant for close scrutiny. Passed over more than once for promotion at several ivy league colleges, he had settled in southwestern Virginia with a chip on his shoulder and a drink in his hand. Once an attractive man with a bright future, he now had two bad marriages and almost half-a-century behind him.

His scowl was deepening and Lesley could feel her stomach knotting at the coming confrontation. "Well, now that you're here," he began, "I'd like to discuss your failure to obtain the interview I sent you for yesterday." It was just like Gerald to try and gain the offensive even when he was at fault.

"Gerald," Lesley said evenly, "yesterday I was humiliated and treated like a call girl, and I understand that you were at least partially at fault." Her fingernails made deep impressions in the palms of her hand as she continued. "I'm not going to stand for that kind of treatment again."

"Call girl? Isn't that role a bit out of character?"

She winced at the intended insult. "I know the story, Gerald. I'm surprised that you had such little regard for me. I'm prepared to forget it, but next time I won't be so kind."

"What did this Travis Hagen tell you that would give you such a poor opinion of me, my dear?" Lesley noticed the beginnings of a sickly smile. "The man is an insufferable bore. I only wish we didn't have to deal with his kind in this research."

"Yes, it is amazing the kinds of people that one has to deal with in this research," she said sweetly as she met his eyes without flinching. The effort to remain surface-calm made her hands begin to sweat and the salt created irritating sensations in the faint abrasions caused by her fingernails.

Gerald leaned back in his chair as her innuendo penetrated the pounding headache he had been experiencing all morning. "We could manage without you around here, my dear. Don't get too uppity or you'll find yourself out of a job."

Lesley thought about all the hours she put in on the research, all the data she single-handedly had collected, all the ideas that she had incorporated into the study. Gerald knew these things too, and instinctively Lesley knew that her job was perfectly safe. "I could quit, Gerald. I will quit if you ever do anything like this again." Despite her quivering knees, she walked to the door.

"What in the blazes has come over you?" he shouted after her.

"A major attack of self-esteem," she said with spirit, and before her spurt of courage crashed around her, she quietly shut the door behind her, leaning briefly against it.

There were plants that needed watering and mail that needed attention. Lesley took care of the most important details and then left the office, waving goodbye to Sylvia. "I'll be back tomorrow; I'll be at Travis Hagen's house this afternoon." The smile Sylvia gave her held surprise and respect.

Lesley gave herself an hour to make the trip from the university to Travis's house. Although she still carried T.J.'s map with her, she found that she had no need to resort to it. The route had been permanently etched in her mind. The landscape looked friendly and familiar. At the turn in the road where she had stopped to fix her flat tire, she passed the old blue pickup driven by the farmer who had helped her the day before. She waved and tooted her horn at him, not seeing the way his eyes followed her as she sped by.

The marked contrast in her mood today as compared to her mood of the day before was a small revelation. Lesley tried to convince herself that coming out of her morning confrontation as the certified victor was the cause of her good spirits. Instead she had to admit that there was more to it than that. She had discovered that she liked Travis Hagen. She was going to enjoy his company today.

She liked his sense of humor when she wasn't on the wrong end of it. She liked his easy casual way and his surprising gentleness. His apologies had almost completely wiped out her humiliation, and she was beginning to feel that he might be trustworthy. It took a big man to admit he had made a mistake, and Travis was certainly a big man. Still, with innate caution, she was going to reserve judgment.

Lesley honked when she reached the end of his driveway, turning her car to ready it for her eventual ascent. The pleasant warmth of the day coaxed her to leave her jacket in the car, and she rolled up the sleeves of the white blouse as she walked up the path to his house. That morning she had chosen to wear her hair in a long braid instead of the perennial bun and it swung gracefully from side to side as she moved. Travis was waiting for her at the front door.

The white knit shirt he was wearing was unbuttoned to reveal the gold medallion. She noticed how brown his skin looked in contrast. Wishing he weren't quite so good-looking, Lesley greeted him with a smile.

"I forgot the lettuce and tomato. I could show you how to harvest some of the spring greens growing out there, instead." She smiled again at his expression and wondered why his face was so intriguing.

"I ran out of bologna anyway. I'm treating you to something even more spectacular." Travis ushered her in, his hand resting lightly on her back.

The casual gesture was appropriate, but she wasn't sure her response to it was. Yesterday Travis Hagen had chased her through this house; today she was letting herself enjoy his touch. Well-tuned warning bells clanged through her head, and she resolved to be careful.

"Let's eat, I'm starved," Travis said as she followed him into the kitchen.

"Mmm...that smell reminds me of the circus." She sniffed the air appreciatively.

"I'm not serving elephant droppings for lunch. I'm much too advanced a chef for that."

Lesley giggled, wondering at the sound. She couldn't remember having giggled in ten years. "What are we having, Travis?"

"Chili dogs. I told you it was something spectacular."

"Hmm...I haven't had chili dogs since the last time I giggled," she said without thinking.

"Pardon me?" His eyes were warm and he was smiling at her.

"Private joke," she said, smiling back.

Perching on a stool she watched him open the canned chili and pour it in a pot to warm up. She took a deep breath, enjoying the chili smell mixing with the salty tang of the boiled hot dogs. "You know, you could use your microwave and do all of that in one step."

He gestured at the gadgets lining the kitchen counter. "If I ever wanted to learn to use this paraphernalia, I'd have to take a six-week vacation just to read the instruction books. Then I'd have to become their slave, cleaning them, coddling them, talking to them, reading them bedtime stories. The thought boggles my mind."

"An interesting perspective."

"Vivian would have my head if I ever got rid of anything, so I let it sit here and gather dust. She seems to think that if the kitchen is well-equipped, T.J. will eat better when he comes to stay with me."

Once again Lesley noted the pride with which T.J.'s name came into the conversation. "Does it work? Does he eat better?"

"Actually, we eat out a lot when he's here. Even I have to admit that a steady diet of cold cuts and hot dogs is not good for a growing boy." Travis's tone was sheepish and a little sad.

They sat at the counter together eating the hot dogs and drinking Coke. Except for the not unpleasant energy she felt radiating from Travis's body so close to hers, Lesley was relaxed. She was glad to be there. Finishing up his third hot dog, Travis turned his stool to watch her profile as she finished her first.

"I was glad to see you drive up, Lesley. I was half afraid that in the light of day you'd think that coming up here wasn't a good idea."

Aware of the close proximity of his face, she turned only enough to glimpse him out of the corner of her eye. "I don't hold grudges, Travis."

"Did you talk to Fatpork today?"

She made a face at the name. "Yes, Dr. Putfark and I had a brief conversation."

"And?"

"I would say that the situation has been straightened out." She kept her voice noncommittal.

Travis put his hand lightly under her chin and turned her face toward his. "I can't tell you if you mean it with these glasses on." He removed them gently. "Now, tell me if everything's all right."

The surprisingly intimate gesture sent confusion washing through her. She met his eyes. "Everything is fine," she said softly. The physical closeness between them left her feeling strangely elated.

Travis seemed reluctant to end the contact but with a shrug he removed his hand, the tips of his fingers trailing a sensitive path to her bottom lip as he stood up to clear off the counter. "You'll let me know if he gives you any more trouble, I hope."

"I think I can handle this by myself, but I was glad to have your conversation with him to pave the way." She followed him to the sink with her plate. "It's too bad that this unpleasantness erupted. I realize now that Gerald isn't a very stable person. I wish I'd realized it before I ever got involved with him." Too late, she realized how her remark had sounded. There was something about Travis Hagen that made her blurt out the strangest things.

Travis was silent as he washed the dishes by hand with Lesley drying them beside him. Finally he said, "It's none of my business, I know, but I gather from what you just said that there is more to your relationship with Putfark than this research project."

Travis's correct use of Gerald's name was a signal of some new emotion, she thought. "You're right, it is none of your business." She considered how best to correct the impression that she and Gerald were an item without acting as though the possibility was anything to apologize to Travis about.

Travis uttered a muffled curse. "That old goat!"

The vehemence surprised Lesley. She came to Gerald's defense. "It takes two to play that game, Travis. Gerald would have to have my cooperation, you know."

Travis turned and faced her, reaching up to lay a wet hand on her shoulder and turning her slightly. "That man could never understand a woman like you or treat you the way you should be treated. How could you settle for so little?"

Lesley threw the dish towel on the counter, narrowly missing a precariously balanced plate. "What do you know about it, Travis Hagen? You don't know me at all. And look at you standing there in your self-righteous glory after your behavior yesterday!"

He shook his head fiercely. "I'm no fool, Lesley. At least I recognize quality when I see it. If you were my woman, I would think twice before letting you near another man, much less send you to one with my blessing. Gerald Putfark is a fool and an old goat!"

Lesley's mouth dropped open at his words. "I have not appointed you as my protector or keeper, Mr. Hagen. I'm here to do an interview. That's all. How dare you get so...so...personal!"

"I have a feeling 'getting personal' is the ultimate sin in your opinion." Travis thrust his hands back in the dishwater.

"And I have a feeling that, in your opinion, 'getting personal' has about as much meaning as yawning or blowing your nose!" The seconds ticked by as she waited for his reply.

"I will attempt to play this game by your rules," he said finally, pulling the plug and rinsing soap suds down the stainless-steel sink. "I will be polite, casual," he said as he turned and favored her with a disarming grin, "and totally irresistible until..."

"Until what?"

"Until you realize what you're missing by not letting me get personal."

"Travis, your ego is so inflated I'm surprised your feet touch the ground!"

He faced her, leaning casually against the sink. "And you're so baffled by male interest that you can't trust it even when you recognize it."

The fact that he had so quickly come to understand the problem that had haunted her since adolescence was intimidating. Lesley didn't like to think that she was that transparent. She shut her eyes against the blue ones that were still examining her.

"Don't run," Travis said quietly.

Running was another problem she had. She forced her eyes open again and that response seemed to convince him that she was going to stay. "Come on, let me give you a tour of the house, then I'll take you out to my studio. All my files are out there."

Lesley followed Travis through the sprawling building, trying to collect her thoughts and ask intelligent questions while his words still rang in her ears. Again she was impressed by the architecture and distracted by the lack of personal detail. There was room after room of wood and stone and beautiful views. Most of the rooms were sparsely furnished and several of the bedrooms had no furniture at all.

"Travis," she said, feeling a need to make conversation and trying to think of how to phrase her question tactfully. "The house is so large and it seems so empty somehow." She stopped, realizing how her statement sounded. "It's just that it seems so big for one person."

"Well, T.J. is here a lot of the time. He brings his friends to spend the night here as often as Vivian will let him. She has a small apartment and really can't entertain his buddies." They turned down the hall that Lesley recognized as leading to the master bedroom, stopping at the corner next to it. "Here's T.J.'s room."

Travis pushed the door open. It was a colorful jumble of posters, pennants, toys and projects scattered all over. Travis walked inside, picking up a soccer ball and setting it on a shelf, only to have it roll off again. He gestured at a table set up in the corner with a microscope, a chemistry set and some ambitious looking experiments that appeared to be half completed. "Right now, T.J. wants to be a scientist. Nothing is safe from his experimenting. Last month he wanted to be a professional baseball player, preferably for the New York Yankees." He gestured to a picture sitting on the desk.

Lesley picked it up, admiring the curly red hair and the bright eyes underneath the gold baseball cap. "I'll bet that T.J. livens up this house immeasurably."

"He makes my life worth living," Travis said simply.

They went back into the hallway and Travis stopped briefly at the door of his bedroom. He smiled his lopsided smile. "You've been here, as I remember."

She refused to respond, stepping just inside the doorway to look quickly around the room. Ignoring the huge water bed, her eyes caught a painting hanging over the fireplace. She moved closer to examine it. It depicted two people at the beach. The curious thing about the painting was that the two people, a red-headed woman and a blond man, were walking away from the artist. Only the back of their heads and bodies were shown. The painting gave Lesley pause; it created an indescribable loneliness within her. She looked at Travis. "Did you do this?"

He nodded. "How could you tell?"

"I'm not sure. The style reminds me in some way of your comic strip. Don't ask me why."

She backed slowly away from the painting, engrossed by its content. Forgetting to judge the distance, she collided with the water bed frame, stumbling to sit none too gracefully on the mattress. The plop created waves and undulations. She laughed ruefully, trying to stand up. "I could get seasick on this very quickly."

Travis watched her with a smile and then came over to give her a hand. "I'd love to see how long that would take."

Lesley followed Travis through the rest of the house and onto one of the decks. There were built-in benches wrapped around the edges, but no tables, no plants, no pieces of sculpture. The surface was barren, but unlike the house, pleasantly so. The mountains were all that were needed. Lesley stopped for a moment admiring the distant peaks. "There are no words to describe that view."

Travis acknowledged her comment with a quotation.

A mountain is a great, big lump
Sort of like a camel's hump. And if you get close to
the side
you might fall off and hurt your pride.

He laughed at Lesley's puzzled expression. "T.J.'s first poem," he said. "Age seven." They went down the steps of the deck heading toward one of the barnboard buildings.

"My studio." Travis opened the door and motioned her in.

"And here's where you live your life," Lesley murmured. The studio contrasted sharply with the emptiness of the house. Every available inch of wall space was covered with drawings, knickknacks, photographs. There were magazines piled neatly on tables, books crammed solidly into bookshelves, file cabinets of every color lining the walls. The furniture here was sturdy and comfortable but supplemented with pillows and a hassock. A huge desk and drawing table combination sat in a corner by a window. Lesley could see what looked like the beginning of a new episode of "The Family Jones" on it.

"Look around. I'm going to go check a trap I set up in the loft." Travis pointed to a small open room built across the heavy beams above them. Lesley admired the view of muscular thighs and firm buttocks as he climbed the decidedly rickety ladder and disappeared. She wandered around the room, examining the displays on the walls and stopped in front of what looked like an antique pitchfork.

Carved into the handle was the inscription: To Grandpa Silas from the grateful citizens of Amesville, Oklahoma, August 12, 1934. She passed over autographed photographs of celebrities, framed letters from famous and not-so-famous fans.

Stopping again she admired a photograph of Travis. He was standing on a stage surrounded by people and he seemed to be receiving some sort of award. She looked closer. The heavily embroidered western shirt, fancy studded jeans and Stetson that he was wearing in the picture were quite different from the casual clothes that she had seen him in, but he looked no less terrific. She did not recognize anyone else in the picture, but an award on the wall next to the picture confirmed her suspicions. It read: To Travis Hagen, Jordan Hagen and Travis Hagen, Jr. For their consistently accurate portrayal of country life. May "The Family Jones" never die. It was signed: The folks at the Grand Ole Opry.

"Lesley, come up here and see what I caught."

She groaned. "Not a chance. I faint at the sight of blood."

"It's a Havahart trap. The animals go in and spring the trap so that you can catch them alive. Come on up and see this little beauty," he demanded.

Lesley took off the serviceable pumps that she was wearing and ventured up the ladder. The loft was a surprise and she stood halfway up the rungs admiring it. She had expected an attic. Instead there was a comfortable bedroom-sitting room combination. All the furniture, including the bed, was built-in and low-lying. There was a thick cocoa-brown shag carpet on the floor and skylights in the ivory ceiling. The effect was sensual. For a moment Lesley imagined what it would be like to lie on the bed and watch the stars on a clear night, cuddled in the arms of the man she loved.

Travis was sitting on the corner of the bed bent over what looked like a small cage. He motioned to Lesley. "Shh...she's scared." Lesley tiptoed over and sat beside him. Inside the cage was a tiny gray creature with a short bushy tail.

"What is it, Travis? A rat or a squirrel?"

"It's a flying squirrel. They've evidently found a way to get into the loft. I hear the scurrying noises sometimes when I'm working downstairs. At night when I'm trying to sleep I hear them running around." He poked the tip of his finger through the cage, making faint clicking sounds at the little animal.

Lesley thought about Travis's words. She wasn't surprised to hear that he slept here. The little studio was warm and cozy. It was alive with his presence and personality. "What will you do with the poor thing?" she asked finally.

"I'd really like to keep her for T.J. He wants a pet so badly."

Lesley nodded her head. "That's a good idea. She's much cuter than a hamster or gerbil."

Travis stood up lifting the cage by its handle. He shook his head slowly. "I really can't do that though. It wouldn't be fair to T.J.'s mother. Vivian can't keep pets in the apartment where they live, and she doesn't need the competition a pet here would create. I'm going to have to take it far away and let it go."

He started down the ladder and Lesley thought about his words. How many ex-husbands showed so much concern for their former wives? She thought back to all of Travis's references to Vivian. Never once had she picked up any animosity. Why was he so thoughtful? Was he still in love with the woman? The thought gave her pause.

Travis stood at the bottom of the ladder, holding it steady. "Come on down."

Lesley looked at him, the ladder and the skirt she was wearing. "You go put the cage outside and I'll get down by myself."

Travis grinned at her discomfiture. "You're going to cheat me out of standing underneath you watching you come gracefully down that ladder?"

"Definitely." She heard the door slam and she scurried down. She had arranged herself on the sofa with a stenographer's pad and pen when he returned.

Travis stood in the doorway watching her for a long moment. "You know, I almost never invite anyone to see my studio. You're the first person who's been here in a long time."

Lesley felt a pang of pleasure. She raised her eyes to his and smiled shyly. He was allowing her to share a part of him and she liked knowing that he trusted her. "I'm very glad you brought me here."

Travis settled on the sofa next to her in comfortable intimacy and she began asking him questions. She found herself wanting to throw away the dull interview format that Gerald had devised. Travis Hagen was an interesting human being and she began to feel that asking him about his philosophy of family life and his views on different topics that related to the media was a waste of time.

After a half hour of dry interviewing, she sighed and stretched. "My sentiments exactly," he said with a smile. "Look, I think it's only fair for me to get a chance to interview you."

"I'm afraid you'll find that very boring," Lesley said with a sigh. "I've got more I'm supposed to ask you anyway."

"Umm...When I agreed to this interview I didn't realize it was going to be philosophy. I was all set to tell you about my entire life."

"I would find that very interesting." She set down the pad and curled her legs under her on the sofa, shifting to face him. "Tell me all about you."

"Only child. Hell-raiser. Poor student. Would-be artist. Terrific cartoonist. Fun-loving. Divorced father-of-one."

"Travis, come on. Fill in the details. Were you really a hell-raiser? I guess I can believe that. And a poor student? That one's hard to believe. I'll write it all down if you want it to be official." Lesley picked up her notebook again.

"You don't have to write it down. I was an only child. I think my parents had given up hope of ever having kids. I came along late in their lives when they were very occupied with other things. I was left at home a lot with the housekeeper and my grandfather, the Travis Hagen that started 'The Family Jones.'"

"That sounds tremendously lonely." Lesley tried to imagine what it would have been like to be raised that way.

"Not at all." He lounged back on the sofa, hands clasped supporting his head. "My childhood was fantastic. Miss Babs, the housekeeper, was a warm and wonderful lady. And my grandfather was the finest man that has ever lived. My parents were fine people too, just not terribly available."

"It sounds like you were raised by Miss Babs and your grandfather."

"With a little help from mom and dad. Anyway, even then I was totally charming and humorous. I got into scrapes constantly, but I had lots of friends. I got kicked out of private school in eighth grade and my parents reluctantly sent me to the local public school. I loved it." Travis looked at her with his lids at half-mast not quite covering a lecherous sparkle. "I discovered girls there. It was quite a discovery."

"I'll bet."

He grew serious. "I met my best friend there too. Joshua. We raised a lot of hell together. Joshua was the brightest, most attractive, craziest human being that ever lived. We went to college together, joined and quit the same fraternity. I majored in art; Joshua majored in having fun." His eyes focused on something beyond the walls of the studio. "When I wasn't out fooling around with Josh, I was busy dating the sweet young things on campus. I met Vivian, my ex-wife, there."

Lesley watched him. Instinctively she waited quietly for Travis to go on. She didn't want to interrupt his thoughts.

"My grandfather died when I was in high school. In college my father had a serious stroke. By then I knew that I wanted to continue 'The Family Jones.' It was in my blood and I guess I was a natural at cartooning. I went home in my senior year to take over the strip. I was going to go back to the university to see Joshua graduate. He was killed in a car accident one month before graduation."

The room was silent. Lesley was left with nothing to say. She put her hand on his shoulder in comfort.

He smiled slightly. "I went back for his funeral. Vivian had been a good friend of Joshua's too. You might say his death brought us together. We got married and went back to New York to live. T.J. was born and we lived together for three years."

"So many losses in such a short time." Lesley's voice was soothing.

"Vivian and I couldn't make it together. We parted as good friends and we have joint custody of T.J. When I looked around for a place to move to, we selected southwestern Virginia as a good spot for us. We wanted to be close enough so that T.J. could spend lots of time with us both. Vivian has a business in Roanoke, and I have my studio here. The end of my life history."

Lesley realized that her hand was still on Travis's shoulder. She removed it discreetly. "I can see why T.J. is so important to you. You've lost so many people you loved." They sat quietly together.

Travis finally turned slightly to face her. "I really don't usually burden people with my life story. You're easy to talk to, did you know that? Very nice to look at and very easy to talk to. Thank you for listening."

The unexpected compliment infused her with warmth. "I liked hearing about you, Travis." She looked at her watch. "I think I've taken up enough of your time for today. Will you have a chance to finish this another time?"

He nodded. "I meant what I said about using my files too. Are you still going to need them?"

Lesley slipped her shoes on, stood and smoothed her skirt. "It would certainly make things go faster for me if I could."

"Come up on Friday then. On Friday afternoon I won't be needing the studio and you can have it to yourself." Travis stood and walked with her to the door.

"Thanks for lunch and for the interview."

Travis put a hand on her shoulder, removing the tinted glasses that she had slipped back on at the interview's end. "My pleasure, Lesley."

They stood for a moment in quiet intimacy. Travis had chosen to share his story, and Lesley realized that the simple act had moved them from the awkwardness of casual acquaintances to another more significant plane. Finally he squeezed her shoulder and dropped his hand. She took her glasses and carried them down the stairs without putting them back on. At the bottom she saw the small wire cage. It was empty. Puzzled she looked back up at Travis.

"I didn't have the heart to remove her from her home," he said sheepishly. "I guess I'll have to share my loft with 'The Flying Squirrel.'"

Lesley raised her hand in salute. She had learned more about Travis Hagen today then any interview could possibly reveal. And she definitely liked what she had discovered.

## Chapter Four

With the sharpest butcher knife she owned, Lesley hacked mercilessly at the roots of the fern held tightly in her hand. She had sweated over the major surgery of this one unwieldy pot of rootbound plant for long minutes, finally repotting the divisions into three smaller pots. "There," she whispered to the new little ferns. "All set now."

Satisfaction for a job well done was replaced quickly by dismay. "Now what?" she muttered. There had hardly been room in the tiny apartment for the big pot, let alone three more pots, even if they were smaller in size. Sighing, Lesley moved every plant on her shelf over a fraction of an inch, managing to make room for two of the small pots. The other she set on a saucer on the floor by the sofa. She would have to be sure to rotate them.

While cleaning up the mess, she passed the clock in the kitchen. It was now ten-thirty. Ten-thirty on a Saturday morning and she had already run through her entire list of important and not-so-important things to do. "Terrific," she mourned. "Great. I now have the entire weekend at my disposal."

Mentally Lesley ticked off the possibilities for the long day ahead. She could work on the stuffed dragonfly that she was making as a Christmas present for Jennifer's son, Troy. She could go to the grocery store and shop for several items she might need eventually. She could drive to the National Forest and hike to a waterfall that she particularly liked. She could listen to Rachmaninoff and daydream about Travis.

Two weeks had passed since Lesley's first encounter with Travis Hagen. During that time she had seen him often. His complete cooperation with her research had enabled her to spend countless hours in his studio, reading and analyzing long series of his comic strip. She had become entranced with the little characters who embodied so well the independence and neighborly spirit of rural America.

She had come to know and fall in love with Grandpa Silas and his wife. She had thrilled to the birth of their grandchildren, Bubba and Sally. She had laughed at their antics and felt the familiar pangs of adolescence as she watched them struggle. She had watched in dismay as Grandma Jones faded from the strip and died. She carefully categorized the events. Never losing her researcher's perspective, Lesley still allowed herself to feel the impact of the many-layered messages of the comic strip. Good content analysis was always done with the heart as well as the head.

And as she gave her heart to the imaginary family of Grandpa Silas Jones, Lesley realized that she was fast giving her heart to its creator, Travis Hagen. Under the power of Travis's able fingers, the strip had grown and changed. Travis had added new dimensions, new depths. The stories were alive and full of meaning. And Lesley had begun to realize that her own story was growing and changing too. Unwilling to give a name to her feelings, she still realized that something special, something magical was happening inside her.

Pushing the idea of Rachmaninoff and fantasy to the bottom of her list, Lesley began to consider the other possibilities. She might be taking more than a casual interest in Travis Hagen, but she was no fool. Thinking too much about him was a dangerous game. Travis Hagen was not for Lesley Belmont. Not for her the warm, heavy-lidded eyes, the powerful athletic body, the sensuous smile. She shook her head. Grocery shopping. That's what she needed to do. Nothing would cure this strange languor as quickly as a trip down the aisles in search of salad dressing and drain opener.

The doorbell interrupted her plans; and Lesley felt a surge of relief. Safe the grocery store might be, but interesting it was not. "Who's there?" she asked idly as she opened the door.

"It's the U.P.S. man." Travis stood sedately in the hallway, not even trying to lounge on the doorframe. "I'm here to deliver a proposition to a certain young lady." His voice was comically serious and Lesley pulled the corners of her mouth down, erasing the welcoming smile.

"By all means, Mr. U.P.S. man. Come in. I understand it's against all company policies to deliver propositions standing in the hallway."

Travis walked through the door and looked around the apartment. "I'm checking to see if you have an armed guard in here."

"Pardon me?"

"An armed guard. Any woman who opens her door so willingly without knowing who is waiting outside must have an armed guard protecting her." Travis faced Lesley sternly. "What if I hadn't really been the U.P.S. man?"

"Impossible!"

"I can see that you can't be trusted to stay here alone today and answer the door. Get your things together so I can take you out of this place for your own good."

Lesley smiled up at him now and shook her head. "No, absolutely not. I will not read another comic strip; I will not analyze another comic strip. This is my day off and I don't even want to hear the word comic strip."

"And I was all set to give you a lecture on the history of political expression in the funny papers, starting with 'Little Orphan Annie' and leading up to 'Doonesbury.'"

She made a face at him, hoping that the playful exchange between them had masked her real joy at seeing her favorite comic strip artist on her doorstep. Having Travis there was almost too good to be true.

"Cheeky little thing, aren't you?" Travis brushed Lesley's cheek with his fingers, pinching it lightly. "I can see that you need lessons on submitting to the greater will. Your proper instruction will begin by going with me to see T.J.'s first Little League game of the season."

Lesley ignored the warm rolling shivers racking her body at his casual touch. "Little League...that's baseball, isn't it?"

Travis heaved a huge martyred sigh. "Yes. Obviously you did not grow up with brothers."

"I have a niece that plays on a Little League team, for your information, Mr. Hagen. Not having grown up in such an enlightened generation it will just take some of us old fogies a few years to catch up."

Travis dropped down on the sofa, settling in comfortably as Lesley debated his offer. "You don't happen to have anything left over from breakfast, do you? A piece of toast, a hard-boiled egg?"

She shook her head, grimacing playfully. "A crust of bread, a rotten apple? I guess I can rustle up something for a starving cartoonist." In a minute she came back from the kitchen carrying two cups of coffee and thick slices of banana nut bread.

Travis sighed in pleasure as he bit into the banana bread. "Even though this is obviously teeming with wheat germ and vitamins, it's delicious. The coffee's good too."

"Tell me about the game. It sounds like fun." Lesley admired the strong muscles in his jaw as he savored the bread. Such strong teeth, such sensual lips. Mentally she shook herself, recalling that she had already decided against fantasizing that day.

"T.J.'s team takes on its first opponent this afternoon. He's going to win, of course. I thought you'd enjoy being there for the victory."

Lesley looked at Travis suspiciously. "You aren't the coach by any chance, are you?"

Travis grinned, setting down his coffee cup and stretching his arms over his head, revealing the powerful muscles in his chest and the outline of the ever-present medallion under the gold knit T-shirt. "Assistant to the assistant coach. I live too far away to be at all the practices. But I know a superior team when I see one. Actually T.J.'s their pitcher this year. And of course, I taught him all he knows."

"I guess I'll have to judge for myself." Lesley looked down at the gray housedress that she was wearing. "I'll have to change. What does the well-dressed fan wear to a Little League game?"

"Something cute and sexy, to show off the fan's cute and sexy rump, preferably."

Lesley blinked, coloring slightly. "Excluding that, what's my next choice?"

"I'm perfectly serious. A pair of shorts will do. I brought you a gold T-shirt to wear with the shorts. T.J.'s team has gold uniforms."

"Going a bit overboard, wouldn't you say?"

"I might concede that it's going a bit overboard, but I'll only concede if you wear the T-shirt."

Lesley refused to be trapped. "I don't even own a pair of shorts. I have some knit pants I could wear, I guess."

Travis made a face of undisguised disgust. "Jeans? Hey, I have the perfect solution. I remember you were wearing jeans the last time I was here. Get them and I'll show you my idea."

Lesley rummaged uncertainly through her closet, finally spotting the old faded jeans in the corner. She took them into the living room and dropped them on Travis's lap. "Here, you can see they're totally disreputable."

Travis nodded, pulling a Swiss army knife from his pocket and detaching the scissors from inside the knife. He cut a slit in the jeans, tearing them evenly along the front of one leg, and turned them around, doing the same to the back. The other leg joined the first one on the floor. "There, now you have a pair of shorts."

"Shorts? That looks more like the bottom of a bikini. I can't wear those, Travis!"

Travis stood dangling the shorts under Lesley's nose. "A designer original will not, cannot be refused. Try them on. I'll go outside and get the shirt out of the car." As he turned she saw the words Mom's Kountry Kitchen on the back of the shirt.

"Travis, does the other shirt say..."

He faced her, his teeth flashing white against his tanned skin. "Of course. Mom's the team sponsor." Lesley shrugged her shoulders in defeat as she went into the bedroom. Pulling off the housedress she squirmed into the shorts. There was no question about it. They certainly did spotlight a lot of her cute little rump. Revealed in the mirror, with only her bra and the shorts, she thought there might possibly be something a little sexy about her image. The thought pleased her immensely.

A knock at the bedroom door signaled Travis's return with Mom's fabric advertisement. Lesley stuck her hand through the door and felt the soft knit brush against her fingers as it was held tantalizingly outside her grasp. "Travis," she warned.

An audible, self-sacrificing sigh wafted through the door as the shirt was deposited into her outstreched palm. She grabbed it, shutting the door with a bang. The T-shirt, like the shorts, fit like a second skin. Lesley seriously considered throwing them both in the trash, but the image in the mirror was a trifle too flattering to deny. She had to admit that what she saw was not the same image that she usually projected. The gold of the shirt was a surprise with her skin, and she actually thought she detected some reddish glints in her brown hair. Brushing it quickly she caught it in a simple waving pony tail at the nape of her neck. Taking a deep breath Lesley ventured through the bedroom door.

"I guess I'm ready," she proclaimed shyly.

Travis stood looking at her, his gaze taking in every inch of the obviously curvaceous body. "It's a good thing it's not adult baseball we're watching. No one on the team would be able to concentrate." He took her arm before she could protest his remark. "Come on, we have to pick up T.J."

The trip to Roanoke took almost an hour. Lesley relaxed against the leather upholstery of Travis's Wagoneer. The big silver station wagon was comfortable and purred like a domesticated tiger as it easily defeated the mountain interstate. She had heard that this particular jeep was often referred to as a "country Cadillac" and she believed it. Surreptitiously she watched Travis as he concentrated on the road. He was serious when he drove, not the daredevil she had expected. He stayed strictly to the speed limit and passed only when necessary.

"You don't drive like I expected you to," she commented casually.

He seemed to be thinking about her remark. "My driving habits made an abrupt change after Joshua was killed," he said finally. "He was killed because he was driving while he was drinking. The original wild and crazy guy."

"I'm sorry, Travis," Lesley said, mentally giving herself a hard kick.

"His death profoundly changed my life." The words were weighted, and Lesley sensed a meaning that was beyond her understanding. "Now I don't have more than an occasional drink and I don't exceed more than an occasional speed limit."

The rest of the trip was made in silence, both content to watch the passing scenery. At the first Roanoke exit, they pulled off the interstate, driving through suburban developments and past fast-food establishments and small shopping centers. Travis turned in at a modest apartment complex, parking next to a giant swimming pool. "Come on in with me, Lesley. I want you to meet Vivian."

Lesley hesitated slightly. Travis seemed to sense her uneasiness and smiled with encouragement. "Vivian is not what you'd expect. I want you to meet her."

He got out and came around to Lesley's side, pulling open her door and taking her hand. Once outside the car he didn't let go of it.

"Won't T.J. feel a little odd with me going to his game?" The combination of meeting Travis's ex-wife and the feel of his big hand enveloping hers was producing an attack of cowardice.

Travis chuckled, the rich deep sound causing her to stop momentarily. "Vivian and I have been divorced for a long,

long time. T.J. was very young. He doesn't even remember us being together, and he's always after me to marry again. T.J.'s convinced I need a wife. He tries to marry Vivian off at every opportunity too.''

Lesley continued to let Travis pull her down the sidewalk. The arrangement seemed peculiar to her, but she was willing to go along with this meeting. Besides, she was only here on a casual outing, not to announce marriage plans. Certainly Travis deserved to have friends and she was glad that she qualified as one of them.

Travis's knock was answered by a wiggling, laughing torpedo of red-haired little boy. "Hey mom, dad's here." T.J., wearing a bright gold baseball uniform, grabbed Travis and pulled him into the apartment. Lesley followed shyly, her discomfort increasing as she stepped over the threshold and glimpsed the lovely woman kissing Travis's cheek.

On tiptoes to reach him, Vivian still looked like a petite, exquisite doll. Curly, strawberry blond hair and translucent skin with soft golden freckles were set off by unusual wide-set turquoise eyes. Everything about her was perfect. Lesley recognized the sinking feeling she was experiencing. She had had it before in the presence of beautiful women.

Travis introduced them and Lesley waited for the other woman to react to her. One might be outright dismissal. Another could be exaggerated politeness. A third might be veiled hostility. In Lesley's experience, beautiful women seldom enjoyed interacting with other women of any type, at all.

"Lesley, I'm so glad to meet you," Vivian said warmly, her voice quiet and feminine with just the hint of a cultured Southern drawl. "Travis has told me about you, and I'm so glad you're going to watch T.J. play today. Those two need a cheering section."

Lesley smiled uncertainly. Her mental catalog had missed this response. She had definitely not expected genuine warmth. She had anticipated a put-down and there had not been one. She filed the experience away, deciding that she should evaluate it at a later time.

Vivian offered them iced tea and Travis gratefully accepted for them, in between playful punches he was exchanging with T.J. Lesley spent the time that it took for Vivian to serve the tea to look around at the apartment. The creamy white walls were set off by bright turquoise and gold upholstered furniture. Accents of peachy tones predominated everywhere. The colors were striking together and Lesley admired the warm richness they created.

"I love the colors in here," Lesley complimented Vivian as she came into the room with the tea.

"Thank you. I used the colors from both T.J.'s and my own palette. He's an Autumn and I'm a Spring so we had some colors in common to work with." She set the tea on the maple coffee table in front of them, seating herself next to Lesley.

Lesley was puzzled by the explanation. "Autumn? Spring?"

Vivian laughed good-naturedly. "Travis didn't tell you that I'm a color consultant, did he? I analyze people's colors. I have a salon that specializes in helping people identify what colors they should wear, what colors they should avoid, and how to use them in their daily life. We use a system that categorizes people by the seasons of the year."

Lesley thought about Vivian's comments. "According to when you were born?"

Vivian shook her head. "No, it's not like a horoscope. We analyze your coloring: eyes, hair and skin tones. I'm a Spring because I'm a strawberry blonde and because my skin has a golden undertone. T.J.'s an Autumn because his hair is such a bright red." She turned and studied Lesley for a moment. "I'll bet you're an Autumn too."

Lesley raised her hand to her hair. "But my hair's not red."

Vivian nodded. "Right, but your skin is a nice golden beige color and your hair has a chestnut glow to it. I can't tell you for sure in this light, but I'll bet you're an Autumn. Besides you look great in that color gold. Travis, on the other hand, shouldn't be caught dead in that color. He's a Summer and he's not supposed to wear gold."

Lesley looked closely at Travis. She couldn't imagine him looking bad in anything. He smiled playfully at Vivian. "Do you think you could color coordinate the team uniforms next year, Viv? The coaches would be so grateful. Just the other day I heard them discussing how terrible it was that all those little boys who were Summers and Winters had to wear gold uniforms." He bent his head quickly to avoid the pillow Vivian hurled at him.

"Watch him, Lesley. That sense of humor of his has been known to get him into serious trouble." They sat sipping their iced tea. Lesley watched in fascination as Vivian and Travis carried on a friendly conversation about T.J. and his plans for the coming week. Their relationship seemed to be too good to be true. Anyone watching them would think that there had never been a moment's tension between them. And yet they were divorced.

"Lesley, are you a baseball fan?" Vivian turned to address her and again Lesley marveled at the delicate beauty of Travis's ex-wife.

"I haven't really had a chance to find out. I'm looking forward to seeing T.J. play."

"He's good, I think. But I guess I'm terribly prejudiced. Travis has taught him so much. I just can't make it to all these games so I'm really delighted that you're going to be there." There was no cattiness in her statement.

Picking up the iced tea glasses she walked gracefully into the kitchen. Lesley's eyes followed her movements, and then turned to watch Travis wrestling with T.J. on the floor.

How could anyone lose Travis Hagen and be so casual about it? Lesley couldn't imagine Vivian feeling so comfortable with his relationship with another woman. Of course, Lesley knew she would be no competition for Vivian, but the strange part of the whole thing was that Vivian didn't seem to be at all concerned. Here was one of the most attractive men ever, and she had let him slip through her fingers somehow. Why, Lesley wondered. And Travis, although friendly and concerned, seemed to have no interest in Vivian. Lesley, an expert at picking up on undercurrents in relationships had detected none between Vivian and Travis.

"Let's go, Lesley. It's time to get T.J. there for pre-game warmup." Travis took Lesley's arm and walked with her to the door, pushing T.J. along in front of them. Vivian came out of the kitchen to say goodbye, kissing T.J. and wishing him good luck. "Goodbye, Lesley. I'm glad I got to meet you. Enjoy the game." They were out the door and down the stairs, Lesley still trying to piece together the curious meeting.

T.J. wiggled and chattered all the way to the ballfield. Like his mother he was genuinely nonchalant with Lesley, seeming to accept her as a friend of his father's. He pointed out his school to her as they drove past, and told her about some of the friends that went there with him. Red-haired and freckled, he didn't resemble his father in the least, although Lesley caught an occasional expression that was pure, unadulterated Travis Hagen.

Waving goodbye to T.J., who had jumped from the car and sprinted to the ballfield as they parked, Lesley and Travis bought Cokes and hamburgers at the little stand by the bleachers and settled down to wait for the game. Travis draped his arm casually around Lesley's back as they leaned back against the row of seats behind them. The May sunshine beamed down on them with mild intensity. She was glad that she was wearing shorts.

"T.J. is quite a mover, isn't he?" She watched him running all over the field, pitching, catching, fielding, all with apparent ease.

"T.J. has Vivian's evergy. He never sits still."

"He must get it from Vivian. I don't recall seeing you move that fast ever." Lesley looked at Travis, conducting a survey of his features to see how he took her comment.

"You, my dear, have no idea how fast I can move if I think it's prudent to do so." His arm tightened around her neck, sending a shiver down her spine.

The game began with T.J.'s team in the field, and T.J. was pitching the first inning. Travis and Lesley sat quietly watching the game unfold. As more parents came to sit on the bleachers, Travis introduced her to them. The group quickly developed a rowdy camaraderie, yelling instructions to their children, cheering for the team, and hooting at calls from the umpire that didn't agree with their perceptions. Lesley found herself getting caught up in the excitement. When T.J. pitched a no-hitter in the third inning she stood and cheered with the others.

Travis was like a different person. Shouting and clapping with the spectators, he left periodically to talk with the coach and to give careful instructions to T.J. who seemed delighted to have the attention. Never angry or belligerent, Travis still exhibited an intense interest in the outcome of the game. Lesley was surprised to see how involved he was in the whole affair.

A voluptuous, bordering on plump, brunette sitting in the bleachers began asking Travis for advice about her son's fielding. The boy, a decidedly overweight rightfielder, seemed to have very little energy or skill. Travis politely gave her some tips as he kept his eyes on the progress of the game. Lesley noticed the batting of eyelashes, the breathy voice, the way the woman moved closer to Travis as she talked. Travis seemed to be oblivious to all the signs of the flirtation, although the arm draped around Lesley's shoulder tightened its hold, pulling her closer. She was gratified and relieved when the woman sat back resentfully to watch the game.

The game was tied in the final inning when Mom's Kountry Kitchen came to bat. The chatting in the bleachers stopped as the first little boy struck out. T.J. was on deck and Travis was breathing heavily. "My stomach drops a foot every time this happens," he said softly. He grasped Lesley's hand, gripping it tightly. She covered it with her free hand. Neither of them took their eyes off the field.

T.J. stood at the plate, making a few practice swings. Although he was a talented pitcher, even Lesley, for all her inexperience, could tell T.J. was not the best batter on the team. The first pitch went past him and the umpire called a strike. The second pitch was barely out, and correctly identified as a ball. Two more balls were followed by a strike. "God, I hate this part of it," Travis shuddered next to her.

The pitcher wound up; T.J. swung the bat and connected with a resounding hollow sound that filled the little park. Dropping the bat he ran the bases, picking up an extra base on an overthrow and landing on second easily. Two more hits by his teammates and T.J. slid into home plate, scoring the winning run. Travis and Lesley jumped up from their seats grabbing for each other with big hugs and shouts. "Lesley, I think I lived through that because of you." Travis slid his hand down her back, pressing her against him and kissing her with all the pent-up energy he had reserved for the celebration.

Lesley watched Travis run down the steps to congratu-
late T.J. and his team. It was a casual kiss, she told herself. He was excited; it meant nothing. Still the feel of it
lingered on her lips as she followed slowly behind, catching a glimpse of the overblown brunette who was giving
her a malicious stare.

"I told the coach we'd take half the team over to Dairy
Queen for ice cream, is that all right with you?" Travis was
standing next to the dugout when she reached him, trying
to round up T.J. and friends as they danced around him.

"Sure, I want to hear all about the game from the real
heroes here," she said as she picked T.J.'s hat up off the
ground and plopped it back on his head.

Turning to smile up at Travis she caught a satisfied look
on his face as he took her arm. "I thought you'd be a
trooper," he said simply. The small compliment gave her
a warm glow as they walked to the car with seven boys
running ahead of them.

Hours later, Lesley stood with Travis in front of her
apartment door. "It's been a lovely day; I enjoyed seeing
T.J. play." Waiting a second for Travis to say goodbye she
realized that he was watching her closely. With his arm
propped on the wall by her door, his face was close to hers,
creating an enforced intimacy that left her breathing short,
shallow gulps of air.

"Invite me in."

Lesley shyly searched his face. The casual smile was not
there. Travis was regarding her with an intensity that she
had not often seen in his eyes. The change flustered her.
"Are you hungry again? It's been over an hour since you
polished off your banana split, and half of T.J.'s too." Her
voice, to her own ears, did not sound casual or flippant. It
sounded shaky and that realization unnerved her more.
She looked down at her shoe.

"I'm hungry all right." Travis lifted her chin with the fingertips of his free hand. "There are some things that I could never get enough of."

She blinked, wishing suddenly that she was wearing the big dark glasses that had been in her handbag most of the day. Now was the time to put a stop to the flirting, she knew. If she was going to salvage a friendly relationship with Travis, it had to be done now. If this innocent flirting went any farther, one or both of them might be too embarrassed to see the other any more. And with a pang, Lesley realized that not seeing Travis would be devastating. "Travis, don't toy with me. I don't think I could stand it from you. Let's just be friends."

"I haven't toyed with a woman since I was nine years old and I tried to get Miss Babs to let me sneak a puppy into the house. You can't believe I'm really interested in you, can you?" Travis looked genuinely perplexed. "Is a guy who draws comic strips too far below your academic level to be a serious candidate for your affections? Funny, I hadn't thought you were a snob."

Lesley turned her back to him and bent over slightly to unlock the door of her apartment. The elementary task gave her a few moments to calm herself. What was she going to tell Travis? That she couldn't believe that he would really find her attractive? That she was sure such a tremendously appealing man would have his pick of prettier and more interesting women? Lesley could not bring herself to admit these feelings to him. Slowly she opened the door and walked inside, waiting for Travis to follow behind. Instead he remained in the doorway, leaning casually against the doorframe. She turned and watched him, as she contemplated what to do about this snag in their blossoming friendship.

Travis stretched out his hand to touch her face, trailing his strong fingers down her cheek and over her lips. He

cupped her chin gently and raised her head the infinitesi-
mal distance he needed to look in her eyes. "There's so
much hesitation there, I can almost touch it. I don't understand you at all, Lesley, but if you want me to leave you
alone, I will. You've got to tell me what you want though,
if you can."

Lesley stared into the depths of his eyes. There was only
kindness and an answering flicker of the hesitation he had
seen in hers. She considered the possibility that his interest in her might be more than a mindless flirtation.
"Travis, I want to be your friend," she said haltingly.

"And?"

Her heart skipped a beat at the one syllable word. And?
And what? In her wildest fantasies Lesley knew what she
wanted. She was equally sure that if Travis suspected the
intensity of her feelings, the knowledge would be the kiss
of death to their relationship. "And...I don't know...can't
say. Let's not rush anything...." She was breathless and the
words came out with a strangling sound.

A glimmer of humor shone in his eyes. "Well, you
didn't say much, but I'd say you were very expressive." He
continued cupping her chin as he moved closer, moving his
other hand slowly around her back, under the soft knit of
the T-shirt. The strength of his fingers caressing the soft
pliable flesh under the shirt sent electricity jolting through
her body, and she moaned in answer as his mouth came
down to claim hers.

"Is this rushing you?" Travis asked lifting his mouth
from hers for an instant. He ran his tongue along the bottom lip and when she sighed as she relaxed against him, he
kissed her harder, moving his tongue slowly into the sweet
warmth of her mouth. His hand found the clasp of her bra,
easily unhooking it as he pulled her closer against him.
"And this, is this rushing you?" he murmured into her
cheek.

His hand and tongue sent wild shivers through her, shivers that she was sure he felt. The strong fingers caressing her came around to cup the softness of her breast, slowly, ever so slowly finding their way to the soft crest, which was no longer soft, but hard, seeking the warmth of his fingers. "Travis," she said shyly, trying to pull away.

"Yes, Lesley? Am I rushing you?" His arm easily held her next to him, his body hard and strong against hers. He covered her mouth, ignoring her murmured protests. His hand found her other breast and caressed it, tantalizing the peak until it too was aching with need for him. Finally, pulling back slightly, he looked at her, the ever-present glint of humor mixed with a smoky desire that Lesley recognized with wonder. "Funny, I could swear you enjoyed that, rushed or not."

She pulled back, humiliation pinkening her cheeks. "Don't make fun of me Travis Hagen!"

"Never, Lesley." Anger replaced the humor and wiped away any trace of the desire. "Why don't you stop looking for people to make fun of you? You're an attractive, fascinating woman. Why on earth do you always think I'm just playing with you? Did that Putfark clown run a steamroller over your ego?"

Lesley turned to shut the door, her emotions churning and hot tears threatening to spill over. Travis grabbed her hand. "I'm sorry, that was out of line." He raised her hand to his mouth, kissing her fingertips as she tried unsuccessfully to pull them away. "I intend to see you soon." She heard the door click behind her as the tears began to fall.

Sitting on the sofa she briefly gave way to the storm of emotions she felt, weeping with the abandon of a small child. Tears fell for all the empty lonely years she had spent afraid to risk rejection to pursue love. Tears fell for the mistakes she knew she was making with Travis Hagen.

When the storm was over she began to let her mind drift on the events of the day. Strangely she felt cleansed by the tears as the day is cleansed by a passing rainstorm. A peaceful feeling began to steal over her.

Travis was right. Once again she had allowed her shyness and lingering feelings of inadequacy to take control of her life. Since she had know him, her insecurities about her impact on men had become painfully evident. And the reason was that she had found something that was worth stepping outside her comfortable and safe little world for. In order to get what she truly wanted she was going to have to risk herself. She was going to have to risk rejection, failure, pain. With no promise of reward. With no assurance of success.

Travis Hagen was worth it. That much she knew. But did she have the courage to suffer the devastation that losing him could bring? Would it be better just not to try? Today he had made it apparent that he intended their relationship to be something more than a casual friendship. She no longer had that alternative to hide behind. There had been a subtle ultimatum issued and she knew what it was. They could continue their relationship and let it develop as it eventually would, or Lesley could call a complete halt to it now.

Lifting her chin slightly, she wondered if all the people who subscribed to the philosophy that "it was better to have loved and lost" still felt that way after they had lost everything. Lesley had a feeling she was about to put herself in the position of finding out.

# Chapter Five

I sympathize with Garfield the cat. Mondays are definitely the worst day of the week." Sylvia stretched her arms over her head, making no attempt to stifle the huge yawn welling up inside her. Her gray hair and square chin shook with the effort.

Lesley laughed, nodding her head. "I never had any appreciation for the comic strips until I started this project. Now I wonder how I got along without all that homey wisdom."

"See if you can dredge up some homey philosophy to get you through the day, honey. I see Dr. Gerald R. Putfark coming up the walk and he looks fit to be tied!"

Lesley turned in time to see the front door of the little building slam and to witness the stormy entrance of her boss. Gerald, never one to be perky and cheerful in the morning, looked like death warmed over. With a touch of malice Lesley smiled sweetly. "Good morning, Gerald. Isn't it a lovely day to be alive?"

The slam of the door of his office was answer enough and Lesley and Sylvia exchanged muffled spurts of laughter. "Lesley," Sylvia admonished with a wink, "give that poor man a break. Ever since you told him off that day, he hasn't been the same sweet man we all knew and loved."

Lesley stopped laughing and looked at Sylvia carefully, searching her face for clues. Finally she sighed. "You heard?"

"How could I help it, honey? Dr. Putfark has a voice like a bullfrog when he's mad. And you, well your sweet little voice was raised a few times that day too, if I recollect correctly." Sylvia reached out her hand and covered Lesley's. "We were all cheering for you, in case you haven't figured it out."

"All?"

"Well, a couple of V.P.I. graduate students were here during part of the scene if I recollect correctly."

Lesley shivered in embarrassment. "I guess the story is all over their campus and ours."

Sylvia laughed. "Don't you worry yourself about it, Lesley. Every person that knows him wants to see Gerald R. Putfark get his comeuppance. You're practically a folk hero."

"Gerald really has been worse than usual, hasn't he?" Lesley's voice held a trace of real concern. Gerald's true character had been revealed to her during the unfortunate episode with Travis, but Lesley still harbored the compassionate feelings of one human being for another. Gerald was a man with a multitude of problems and she felt sorry for him.

"Lesley, if you don't mind me saying so, the only time that Gerald Putfark has ever acted like anything but a skunk was when he sobered up briefly to pursue you when you first came to work here. You bring out the best in people." Sylvia turned back to her typewriter. "I'd better get busy or he'll come out and fire me for doing nothing."

Lesley, flushed by the unusual compliment, turned to go to her office. Her desk was covered with papers, her filing cabinet was piled with information to be filed, her plants were wilting from lack of attention, and a thin coat of dust covered all the little knickknacks that she had set around to make her office look more interesting.

The extensive research she had been doing using Travis's files was over and it was time to get back to the segments of the project that could be done in her own office. Lesley felt a sharp twinge of regret. Seeing Travis almost every day had been marvelous. They had lunched together, taken occasional walks up the mountain paths by his house, and indulged in long conversations and poignant silences. She had not heard from him on Sunday after their day at the ballgame. Perhaps he had been permanently turned off by her attempts to keep their relationship on a purely friendly basis. Although Travis's withdrawal might make her life safer, Lesley fervently hoped he would be back.

An hour later, her office was back in order. Even the plants had begun to respond to her ministrations and were busily filling their stems and leaves with the water sitting in their saucers. Lesley was just beginning to sort her research into piles on her desk when the door of her office flew open, and Sylvia poked her head in. "Lesley?"

"Come in." Lesley sat back and sighed. "Have you come to rescue me from all this data?"

"In a manner of speaking, I have. Gerald told me to tell you that he's adding two more strips to the study. He wants you to go to Roanoke and use the microfilm at the library there. It's the only library in the area that has the strips."

Lesley's mouth twitched. "Are you going to carry messages for us from now on?"

"It looks like it. Evidently Dr. Putfark has declared a cold war around here." Sylvia bustled over to the desk and dropped the information on it. "At least this will get you out of the office for the day."

"Well, that's good for me, but it leaves you at his mercy."

"Now honey, haven't you ever noticed how easily I handle the good doctor? Let's just say that Gerald and I understand each other."

The ringing phone interrupted Lesley's laughter. Sylvia reached for it. "Christiansburg College Department of Mass Communications. Miss Belmont is right here." She handed the phone to Lesley with a loud stage whisper. "No luck, it's a woman's voice."

Waving Sylvia out of the room, Lesley picked up the receiver. "Hello?"

The voice at the other end was curiously familiar and Lesley was surprised to hear Vivian identify herself. "Vivian, how are you?" Lesley was at a loss for anything else to say.

"Fine, thank you, Lesley. I was calling to tell you that I enjoyed meeting you the other day, and I was wondering if there was any chance that we could get together for lunch sometime this week? I can drive down there or we can meet half way if you'd like." Her voice was lovely and warm, and Lesley kicked herself for trying to pick up any negative overtones.

"I'd like that, Vivian. I'm going to have to be in Roanoke anyway, today. Could we have lunch then?"

They made a date for one o'clock at the Hotel Roanoke and Lesley hung up wondering what purpose there would be in the meeting. Instinctively she found it hard not to trust Vivian. But she had been wrong about people before. Take Gerald, for instance.

The Hotel Roanoke sat on a knoll overlooking the medium-sized city. Constructed of wood in the Tudor style, the building was imposing and emanated a spacious grandeur. Lesley knew a little of its history. It had been conceived and built a hundred years before when Roanoke was still "Big Lick." Its purpose had been to turn Roanoke into a growing railroad town. Handsomely appointed with hand-rubbed exotic hardwoods, crystal chandeliers, and floor polished to shine like glass, it was a grand hotel.

She parked her car and walked beneath the maroon and tan canvas awning over the front door, admiring the huge circular fountain surrounded by brightly colored tulips. Inside the lobby she sat in a comfortable chair enjoying the atmosphere created by the fine oriental rugs, antiques and fresh flowers.

A few minutes later Lesley looked up from examining the intricate design of a carpet to see Vivian walk through the front door. Dressed in a rich violet shirtwaist dress that somehow accentuated her lovely hair, Vivian was charm itself. Lesley looked down at the navy blue suit she was wearing with dawning distaste. She wished that she had taken the time to go home and change, but the truth was that she had nothing more interesting to change into.

"Lesley." Vivian came over and dropped casually into the chair next to her. "I'm sorry I'm late. I had a woman in the salon today who insisted that only I could do her justice. I hadn't expected such adulation or I'd have told you one-thirty."

"That's quite all right." Lesley assured her, then added, "What a lovely dress. That color looks stunning on you."

Vivian smiled with seemingly genuine pleasure. "Do you like it? I have to admit, I've known for a long time that I was supposed to be able to wear this shade, but I haven't had the nerve until recently."

They chatted comfortably for a few moments and then Vivian led them to the Regency Room where they found a table next to one of the luxuriously draped windows.

"I love it here. You don't expect to find such a first class establishment in a little city like Roanoke. I always pretend I'm dining in Europe," Vivian confided.

"I'm afraid that this is as close to Europe as I've come yet. I have a secret desire to do the grand tour someday." Lesley admired the menu, deciding to take a break from salads for a change.

"I went for a month several years ago. Travis took care of T.J., and I spent the whole glorious time in France and Italy going to cathedrals, art museums, all the really colorful places. And of course, to the fashion houses in Paris. I got some very enlightening viewpoints there." Vivian put her menu down and smiled at Lesley. "I'm lucky that I have Travis to help with T.J. Can you see T.J. in an art museum?"

Lesley smiled at the thought. "In about ten years maybe."

"Exactly."

Lesley ordered an entrée that was guaranteed to put at least four unwanted pounds on most women. Vivian ordered the salad and iced tea.

"I knew it, you're one of those women who can eat anything you want. I could tell the first time I looked at you." Vivian pulled the corners of her mouth down in a pout. "It's not fair at all."

Lesley's eyes widened in surprise. "Well, I never thought much about it. I guess I never had to. But you're gorgeous, and slender too. You don't have to worry, do you?"

"Do you know why I'm sitting on this side of the table?"

Lesley shook her head.

"So that I don't have to look at that cart of pastries over there. If I stare at them I'll gain an automatic ten pounds."

Lesley found herself relaxing. It was hard to remain wary around a woman who could admit to a problem with such candor. "It's delightful to know that I have a hidden asset."

"Really, you're so lucky. I grew up as a hopelessly fat, redheaded kid who was dressed eternally in shocking pink because my mother heard somewhere that pink was flattering with red hair. She decided to prove it to the world."

"Your mother and mine would have been friends. I still hate pink."

Vivian examined Lesley carefully in the light from the window. "That's smart. I still think you're an Autumn, and Autumns should not wear pink, not ever."

In spite of herself, Lesley was fascinated by Vivian's knowledge and she asked tentatively, "What else does an Autumn avoid?"

Vivian hesitated and then said truthfully, "Navy blue."

Lesley sighed. "There goes half my wardrobe."

"And gray...and black...and anything with blue undertones."

"There goes the other half of my wardrobe."

Vivian covered Lesley's hand for a moment. "Cheer up, you still have that terrific gold T-shirt I saw you in on Saturday. Now that's one of your colors." The two women laughed companionably and began to eat their lunch.

Finishing the meal with coffee, Lesley looked at her watch in horror. "It's really getting late. I've kept you much too long."

"Not at all. In fact, I was wondering if you'd like to come to my salon and see what we do. I've scared you with all my chatter about what not to wear, but I'll bet you'd love to see what you can wear. I'll do a consultation for you."

Lesley hesitated. Scrutinizing herself that carefully, especially next to Vivian, did not sound like a good idea. Vivian refused to accept "no" for an answer, however. "Come on, you'll enjoy it. It's fun to see how good colors can make you look. And if I can get away with this outrageous violet dress, just think what you'll be able to wear."

Lesley followed Vivian's car through the streets to a local shopping mall. The shop, "The Rainbow Connection," was sandwiched between a Radio Shack and a local department store. Parking in the large lot, she trailed into the salon behind Vivian, who was excitedly talking a mile a minute. "Come meet my consultants, Marilyn and GeorgeAnne." Lesley was introduced to the two women, who were totally different in looks and coloring from Vivian and from each other. Marilyn was a dramatic looking black woman dressed in a a ruby-red caftan worn with brilliant gold jewelry. GeorgeAnn was a silvery blonde with blue eyes and pale skin. She was wearing a powder-blue skirt and blouse.

"Jeri isn't here today. She's our Autumn. We're all different seasons, and I like to have a woman consult with someone who shares her season when we get around to helping select clothing."

Lesley was surprised. "You select clothing too? What else do you do?"

"A little of everything, really. Help select makeup colors, give advice on hairstyles, shop for clothing. I'm going to expand soon so that I'll actually be carrying clothes in my own store. And eventually we'll have our own hairstylist in the shop too. Someday I'm going to start my own chain."

Lesley followed Vivian to a room in the back of the shop with white walls and lots of windows letting in natural light. "Have a seat, Lesley. I'm going to give you some makeup to put on. Just a little lip gloss and blusher."

Lesley used the gloss and blusher, peering in the mirror to determine what effect it had. She was feeling embarrassed by all the attention, but her academic curiosity and feminine instincts had been aroused. "There." She scrutinized herself carefully. "I don't like it."

Vivian winked at her in the mirror. "Good eye. That's the color you should wear if you are a Winter." She brought Lesley some cold cream and watched her remove the makeup. "Try this now."

Lesley put on the mocha-colored lip gloss and the dark peach-toned blusher. She was sure she would see another mistake. Instead the warm colors flattered her immensely and made her own coloring spring to life. "Wow, what a difference!"

Vivian handed her the cold cream. "I'm convinced I was right about you. You are an Autumn. Let's begin by draping some colors. Take off your jacket. Your white blouse will be a good backdrop."

Vivian reached underneath the counter for a large pile of fabric swatches. She took the top one, a delicate pink, and lay it up next to Lesley's skin. "Shades of my childhood," Lesley said as she made a face.

Next Vivian put a blue-red swatch under her chin. "What do you think of this?"

"It makes me look faded, mousier somehow."

"Mousey, not mousier!"

"Whatever," Lesley murmured.

A bright orange was next. "Never. I'll look like a pumpkin." Lesley tried to ward off the fabric with an outstretched hand.

Vivian stuck out her tongue. "Try it, you might be surprised."

The color was a surprise. It warmed Lesley's skin, making it look clear and alive. "It's not bad, but I'd never feel comfortable in it."

"Like me with my violet dress. It might take a while for you to get used to, but there are plenty of other colors you can start with."

Navy-blue up next to Lesley's skin did make her look sallow. She wondered why she had never figured that out herself. And there were so many shades of navy-blue. Clear-navy, grayed-navy, true-navy, and light-navy. None of them were any good, she decided.

"Why didn't I know all along that these colors weren't any good for me? It seems pretty obvious now."

Vivian was getting more swatches. "I think people buy whatever they're used to seeing on other people. And occasionally we really fall in love with a color that isn't right for us. I have always adored bright ruby-red. Probably because it was so obviously wrong for me. Travis loves lime green. I've had to grit my teeth a few times to keep from rescinding his visiting rights on the days Travis wears a favorite green shirt of his."

Lesley was surprised by the cheerfully casual mention of Travis. She found that she couldn't help herself. "You and Travis are good friends, aren't you?"

Vivian was holding up swatches in the Spring group, showing Lesley how their light tones were too pale for her more earthy coloring. "Yes, I know it's quite surprising. To be honest, that's part of the reason I called you today."

Lesley waited as Vivian bent over to get a packet of material marked "Autumn." "Vivian, I didn't mean to make it sound as though there was anything wrong with your being friends. I hope I didn't offend you."

"Not at all. In fact I'm surprised you're as cordial as you are. I'm afraid that many women would be acting like I was the other woman about now." She began to hold up the Autumn swatches and Lesley was fascinated by them and by the conversation.

"I don't think I'm in any position to worry about the other woman, Vivian. Travis and I are just friends."

Vivian stopped, draping a lovely rust color around Lesley's neck and stepping back to admire it. "That's got to be one of your best colors right there. Isn't that terrific?" She reluctantly removed it, draping a series of olive-toned green swatches and watching their effect. "You may think that you and Travis are just friends, but I suspect you're kidding yourself. He's very interested in you. He's never brought anyone to meet me or to meet T.J. in all the years we've been divorced."

Lesley was astounded by the intimacy of the conversation. She found that she could not retreat casually. "Isn't this a peculiar talk for us to be having? You seem to feel very positive about my having a relationship with Travis. I can't help but wonder why."

Vivian smiled warmly at her. "I don't blame you at all, Lesley, in fact I'm amazed at my nerve for even bringing this up. But the fact is that I desperately want Travis to be happy. And I think that you make him happy." She stopped for a moment and came around in front of Lesley, sitting on the counter under the mirror. "Our divorce was painful and so was our marriage. In fact the circumstances leading to our marriage were also painful. Travis Hagen is one of the most spectacular men alive and I wish more than anything that I could have been the one to bring him joy. But I'm not the one, and I think you are."

There was a heavy silence. Finally Lesley said, "I don't know what to say."

Vivian reached over and squeezed her hand. "You don't have to say anything. When the time comes, tell Travis that I have given him permission to explain our marriage to you. It might clear up a few things."

Lesley watched the color selections unfold. Warm browns and beiges, bronze tones, golds and many different oranges. Muted yellow-greens, a few special shades of blue. She was delighted with the possibilities and mystified by the conversation. Vivian was putting such a strong emphasis on her relationship with Travis. Was it possible that he was really interested in her? As more than just a casual friend to have fun with? As more than just a casual affair?

The door opened and GeorgeAnn came into the room. Vivian motioned her over to stand behind Lesley. "Lesley, GeorgeAnn is our resident expert on hairstyles. GeorgeAnn, what do you suggest for Lesley's hair?"

Coming to Lesley and taking the pins and rubber band out of the bun she wore, GeorgeAnn lifted the heavy hair, feeling its weight and judging its curl. "I'd suggest she give me some of this gorgeous stuff. I could sure use some of this delightful wave." She pulled Lesley's hair straight back from her forehead, revealing the widow's peak that made it so difficult to part. "Shame on you for covering up this wonderful widow's peak. You should never part your hair. Pull it straight back, like this, maybe up on top of your head, or better yet, get it cut and shaped a bit so that you can stop fighting the curl. With a layered cut it will fall around your face and be easier to take care of."

Vivian and GeorgeAnn continued advising her on her hair, makeup, clothing styles. Lesley had the same distinct feeling that she got when she had just gone through an intensive physical at her doctor's office. There was nothing sacred about her anymore. But strangely, the two women had put her totally at ease and she found that she was enjoying the attention. For once, in the presence of two beautiful women, she didn't even feel shy. Both GeorgeAnn and Vivian made her feel attractive. They were only seeking methods to increase her beauty, not change her into something she was not.

Vivian took a hairbrush and pulled it through Lesley's long hair, lifting it high off her neck and fastening it in a coil on top of her head, pulling out a few shorter tendrils to curl softly around her face. Lesley liked the change. "I'll give you the name of a hairstylist who works with us, if you ever decide to take GeorgeAnn's advice." She reached down and pulled out a small swatch of colors and presented them to Lesley. "These are for when you go shopping next."

Lesley stood up wrinkling her nose at the navy blue jacket as she pulled it on. Vivian laughed. "Just start small, Lesley. One thing at a time. Figure out what you have and what you need most and go from there. Buy clothes that are closest to your face first; they're the most important." Vivian walked with her to the front door of the shop.

"I'm glad you called me, Vivian. I've really enjoyed this." Lesley paused thoughtfully. "You realize, of course, what an unlikely fairy godmother you are?"

Vivian arched her eyebrow. "Come again?"

"You're an unlikely fairy godmother. I feel like Cinderella after that experience, and you're the fairy godmother."

A warm smile covered Vivian's delicate features. "I think I like that role. Yes, I think I like that role a lot." Spontaneously she reached over and gave Lesley a hug.

Lesley was touched by the embrace. She left for the library feeling like she had made a new friend and wondering how on earth it had happened.

And how had it happened that Travis Hagen was interested in her? Driving back from the library late in the afternoon she watched the scenery flashing by, scarcely thinking about where she was and what she was doing.

Was Vivian sincere about Travis's attraction to her? Why? "Why" was the question of the day, she decided as she pulled her car into the small parking area beside her apartment.

She opened the door to the stairs leading up to her apartment to find Travis sprawled comfortably on the steps, his body propped on his elbows and his long legs crossed casually in front of him.

"Hello there. I was just in the neighborhood and I thought I'd drop by for a few minutes." Rising, he stepped to one side, propelling Lesley forward with a strong hand.

She unlocked the door and he followed her inside. "What were you doing in the neighborhood, Travis?" she asked inanely.

"Looking for you, of course." The edges of his mouth curled lazily upward. "Surprised?"

"Delighted," she admitted. There was a short pause as they measured each other. Lesley searched his eyes. "I really am glad you came to see me. I acted like a scared rabbit on Saturday."

Travis draped his arm around her shoulder and pulled her over to the couch, sitting comfortably close to her. "Just what is it that scares you about being with me? Am I such a terrifying person?"

"I'm shaking in my boots," she said, only half-kidding.

Travis pulled her around, bending his head as he began to nuzzled her neck. "Mmm...I love terrorizing lovely young innocents. It's every man's fantasy." His tongue teased the velvety hollow at the base of her throat, darting in and around the shallow recess. "Eat a virgin a day, that's my motto." His mouth moved up to her ear, his teeth lightly tormenting the tender earlobe.

"You're going to be awfully disappointed then when I tell you that I am not about to be your dinner." She gasped as his tongue sought the inside edge of her ear, lightly following the curve of it. Her head moved slowly in unconscious rhythm to the sweet caress.

"That's a shame because you are by far the sweetest, most innocent young thing I have ever met." His hand began to rove gently down her shoulders to her breasts, stopping in exasperation at the lapels of her suit jacket.

"Tell me, Lesley. Why do you wear so many clothes? Are you absolutely determined to keep the world from admiring this gorgeous body?" He unbuttoned the jacket, slipping it back over her shoulders only to be confronted with the buttons of the blouse underneath. "Let me guess, under this blouse is at least a full slip and a bra too, right?"

"Travis!" she protested.

He groaned, pulling the jacket back around her and contenting himself with the exploration of the soft skin of her neck and cheeks.

"You're so soft, so warm. I dreamed about you last night."

"What did you dream?" she whispered as his tongue circled her earlobe teasingly.

"I dreamed that you threw away all these suits and started wearing that gold T-shirt everywhere."

"With your designer shorts, no doubt."

"Who said anything about shorts? The T-shirt was just right by itself."

"Travis!" she protested again.

"All right, I give up. My days of ravishment are at an end, due to the modern technology of the fashion industry." He sat up and ran his fingers through his hair. "I'm going to have to enter a convent."

"A monastery," she corrected him.

"No, a convent. It would definitely be more fun there. The nuns dress sexier than you do." Travis leaned back, his arm still draped comfortably around her shoulders. "Actually, I have to go in a few minutes and it's going to be hard to leave if I continue to enjoy touching you so much."

"You're very welcome to stay, Travis." Lesley rested her head on his arm, turning to look at him through lowered lashes. Shyly she traced a design from his earlobe to the tip of his nose. "I have the world's nicest head of lettuce sitting in my refrigerator waiting to be eaten."

"I'll pass, I think. I really came to say good-bye for a few weeks. I'm going to New York to meet with my syndicate. It's going to be business meetings and work on completing my newest episode of 'The Family Jones.' If I weren't going to be so busy while I'm there, I'd ask you to come along."

Lesley let the emotions she was feeling flicker across her face. She was disappointed that Travis was going to be gone but delighted that he had thought of taking her with him. "I'm a working girl, remember? Gerald wouldn't be pleased if I took off for a few weeks anyway."

"Yes, I mentioned it to him today, just to see if I could get his goat." There was a decidedly smug expression on Travis's face, and Lesley sat up straight to look at him.

"Today?"

"I stopped by to see you at work and I got to meet Gerald R. Putfark in person."

"Did you get his name straight?"

"Not one time." Travis pulled her nearer and bent to kiss her, his mouth hovering tantalizingly close to hers. "I don't think Gerald liked me at all."

"I don't think that how Gerald feels about you matters, do you?" she murmured as he moved still closer.

"Right now, there's only one person in the world whose good opinion matters to me, Lesley. Only one." His lips merged with hers, grazing their softness with the firm sweetness of his. Lesley put her arms around his neck, running her hands through the thick tousled hair. She strained closer to him, inwardly cursing the layers of clothing that were keeping them apart. Travis was right, she did overdress!

"After I saw Gerald today, I realized that you weren't involved with him." Travis's mouth was close to her ear, the words were soft and knowing.

"I never said I had been, Travis. You jumped to conclusions, and I didn't think I had to explain anything to you." She pulled away slightly. "Besides, how did you know I wasn't involved just by looking at him?"

Travis was serious, searching her eyes as he answered. "You have too much respect for yourself to let that Putfark character get close to you."

Self-respect was a virtue she possessed, Lesley agreed silently. It was confidence in her ability to attract a man that was lacking. For a moment she let the total extent of her vulnerability pool in her golden-brown eyes for Travis to see.

"It's not just Gerald. I never let anyone get close to me," she whispered.

"Do you understand why?"

She nodded haltingly. "I've always been very serious, taken everything straight to heart. It's part of what makes me such a good scholar and researcher. It's also what makes it hard for me to relax and trust. I'm always checking things out, filing away information, computing statistics."

Travis wound his finger in one of the loose curls framing her face. "You're so busy gathering data that you miss out on the real interactions between people."

"I never miss out if the interactions are between others. It's only when I'm involved that I get worried. I guess I don't trust myself to make a decent decision unless I can isolate a hypothesis, research the subject thoroughly and form a rational conclusion." She wished that Travis would let go of her so that she could avert her eyes, but she knew it was useless to hope he would.

"Life's not like that. Love's not like that. Sometimes you just have to drift with the river, do what your feelings tell you to." He began to caress her cheeks with his thumbs as he continued to tilt her head in line with his.

"I don't want to be hurt."

"No one does."

Shutting her eyes seemed to be the only escape as she said, "Travis, please don't hurt me."

She felt his hands leave her face and the withdrawal was a sudden ache deep inside her. For a moment she was sure that her insecurities, spoken and real, were too much for him to deal with. Then she sensed his face close to hers. "I can't guarantee I'll never hurt you. You'll have to trust me when I tell you that I'll try my hardest not to."

His mouth hovered over hers and Lesley opened her eyes. He was waiting for her answer. "I'll try too," she whispered as he covered her lips with his.

Finally he withdrew, his breathing faster, his smile boyish, his eyes heavy-lidded. "I think I'm going to go now." He stood, pulling Lesley to her feet. "Walk me to the door," he insisted.

At the door Travis pulled her close again, holding her against him, their heartbeats joining for a moment, arms wrapped around each other. His kiss was agonizingly thorough, promising the world. Stirring desire changed his eyes from the brightest blue to a smoky-gray, and Lesley responded to the change with a fervor that left no doubt about her feelings. At the end of the kiss they clung to each other. "I'll miss you," she ventured finally.

"Good. When I get back we'll celebrate," Travis promised softly. Reluctantly he pulled away and opened the door. "I'll see you in two weeks."

Lesley watched as he took the stairs two at a time. The next two weeks stretched in front of her like a yawning chasm, waiting to swallow and drown her in a sea of boredom. She shut the door heavily, leaning against it, her arms folded in front of her.

Crossing the room she entered the kitchen, opening the refrigerator to peer with distaste at the vegetables there. For some reason she had an unaccountable yearning for a bologna sandwich.

## Chapter Six

There were people cemeteries and there were pet cemeteries. Lesley wondered fleetingly if there was a market out there for plant cemeteries as she dumped the little fern into the garbage can. Maybe people would pay for a nice little piece of earth somewhere to bury their prized houseplants when they went to that big garden plot in the sky. She wrinkled her nose in distaste as she looked at the sickly potted specimens gathered together in her living room like a support group for abused flora. She was only too aware of their problem. Nothing could survive the intense dose of love and caring that she had given them for the past two weeks. Every leaf, every frond, every particle of dirt had been lovingly nurtured, fondly patted, carefully sprayed and watered. She had talked to them, wiped them clean, aired them, rotated them to death. "All right, ferns," she said from a safe distance, "you're on your own for the rest of the week. No more Mr. Nice Guy."

Refusing to stay and gauge the response to her radical decision, Lesley went in the bedroom and flopped face down on the bright blue and gold patchwork quilt covering her bed. She could not remember ever having been this bored in her entire life. She had kept herself busy for the past two weeks, so busy in fact that she had only had to think about Travis during the long nights when she really couldn't manage to provide any busy work for herself. Travis Hagen had moved into her life just as surely as if his tall, powerful body was lying on the bed with her at that very moment. Don't I wish, she thought achingly.

The experience was a brand-new one, and Lesley wasn't at all sure that she liked it. Amusing herself had always been easy. Never having been one to depend on someone else for anything important, she was at a total loss to explain her feeling of displacement since Travis had gone to New York. She knew she was letting herself in for a sad awakening. Perhaps Travis would come back totally uninterested in picking up their relationship. But then, she had to admit, there had been several long, intimate phone calls.

Lesley smiled thinking about them. The first time Travis had called she had been soaking in the bathtub and she had come to the phone dripping wet, with nothing but a large bathtowel between her and total nudity. The situation had been hopelessly erotic and she was sure the heat radiating from her skin resulted in making the bath towel's job of drying her off an easy one. The second call had come when she had been getting ready for bed a week later, and again she had found herself filled with lascivious thoughts. Carrying on a chatty conversation had not been easy. She didn't want to chat long distance. She wanted him there in the flesh and she wanted him, period.

The phone rang shrilly, cutting through her daydreams like an alarm clock on a weekday morning. "I'm back," said the deep male voice on the other end, and Lesley knew that her boredom was over.

Taking a deep breath and bravely clutching her color swatches, Lesley entered the door of the little dress shop. The salesclerk smiled invitingly at her, and came out from behind the desk to offer her services. "I want something special for a dinner date tonight, something...sexy." Lesley was certain that the last word came out in a squeak, but the saleswoman nodded her head approvingly and walked with Lesley to a rack of dresses in the corner. Lesley consulted the swatches and selected three dresses in appropriate colors, putting one back because she found it unappealing. Left with the other two dresses she went into the dressing room and began to try them on.

Several hours and shopping bags later, she stumbled into her apartment. Completely drained, but still glad to be alive, she began to unwrap her purchases. A rusty silk dress with a low draped neckline slithered to the floor. Lesley shook it out and hung it lovingly on a padded hanger. Following close behind was a downy knit oyster skirt and blouse accented with touches of deep forest green. Next came several soft pullover shirts in shades of orange-reds and yellow-greens, followed by a camel skirt, a camel blazer, and a turquoise print shirtwaist dress.

In amazement she looked at all the clothing surrounding her. Her closet was going to be crowded and her bankbook was going to be lighter, but she felt like a success. She couldn't believe that she had bought all these clothes today, and that she liked the way she looked in all of them. She had stood in the dressing room and looked at herself, and the experience had not been unpleasant. She could begin to understand how some women seemed to get hooked on shopping.

With the water running full blast, Lesley opened a bottle of bubble bath that she had received as a Christmas present from Jennifer years before, and poured in a large dose. She settled down into the hot sudsy water, enjoying the sensation of languor it produced. When the water finally got too cold, she reluctantly abandoned the tub and dried off, going into the bedroom to unwrap the new lingerie she had bought at the last minute on her shopping spree.

The lovely peach-colored panties and bra felt silky and cool against her heated skin, and the matching half-slip made her feel feminine and very voluptuous. She stood in front of the mirror, frankly admiring what she saw. She wondered why she hadn't noticed before that she really had a very nice body. I've been working hard to hide it all these years, she thought with wonder. How silly.

The rust silk dress moved across her body, clinging to her and accenting her waist. The neckline plunged frankly between her breasts, hinting at, but not revealing, the delights there. The effect was daring, she thought, not at all like the Peter Pan collars she usually wore. "Good," she said out loud. "It's about time!" She began to brush her long hair, enjoying the sensation. Reluctantly she coiled it on top of her head, pulling a few curls loose as Vivian had shown her. The effect was nice but she made a mental note to see about having it cut. The provocative feel of hair swinging against her neck and Travis's fingers threading through it were sensations not to be missed.

A touch of makeup in the colors Vivian had recommended, a squirt of the cologne that matched her bubble bath, and Lesley was ready. She looked at herself in the mirror and panicked. "My God," she muttered. "That's not me. What in the world have I done?" For a moment she seriously considered not answering the doorbell that was now bleating merrily through the apartment. What would Travis think? Had she lost her mind? The doorbell continued to bleat.

Maybe I could change real fast, she thought, abandoning the idea immediately. Travis would leave before she could get into any other clothes. Maybe she could let him in and then change. She abandoned that idea immediately. Travis would think she was crazy. Reluctantly she walked to the door and after taking a deep breath she opened it. Travis leaned against the door frame, holding a florist's box. For several seconds he leaned there, looking at Lesley appraisingly.

"Forget the convent, you've got it way over the nuns." His smile was lazy and his eyes at half-mast as he pushed away from the door frame, leaning over to kiss her. "You're beautiful. I've missed you."

Trembling with a variety of emotions, Lesley pulled him through the door, abandoning herself to his warm strong arms and melting kisses. "I've missed you too, Travis," she murmured against his suede dinner jacket. She pulled away finally to look at him. Nothing he wore was familiar except for the chain of the gold medallion that was peeking out from under the collar of the soft blue shirt that emphasized the startling color of his eyes. "I've never seen you dressed up. I wasn't sure you even owned a coat."

"And I was sure you didn't own a dress like that. Maybe we bring out the best in each other." Travis kissed her forehead, reluctant to let go of her. "I don't want to go. I'd like to stay here all night and hold you like this."

"We could eat here," she said with her heart flip-flopping. "I think I have something I could fix."

Travis wrinkled his nose briefly. "No thanks, I've had a salad this month already." He handed her the box.

Opening it she found a single creamy camellia. "Travis, how lovely," she said as she lifted it from its nest with faintly trembling hands. She walked to the mirror and fastened the flower to the side of the thick coil of hair. It lent just the right touch, she thought, and she turned to let Travis admire it.

"Let's go," he muttered unceremoniously, ushering her out the door before she could say a word.

"What's the hurry? Do you have a reservation somewhere?"

"The only reservation I have, honey, is about standing here watching you and wondering how I'm going to keep my hands off that lovely body. Your apartment is entirely too intimate."

Lesley, glowing from his comment, slid into the seat of the jeep and snuggled down into the soft black leather cushions. She turned slightly to watch Travis as he got in and started up the big car, expertly backing it out of the parking space in front of her apartment. "Where are we going?"

"There's a little lodge tucked away in the mountains just north of Roanoke. It's a long drive, but I thought it would be fun. The food's terrific and the grounds are wonderful for moonlight strolls. How's that sound?"

Privately Lesley thought that Travis could make a fast-food hamburger sound like fun to her. "Perfect," she answered.

The hour's drive went quickly with Travis describing his trip and Lesley telling him about the progress of her research. She was surprised to find them falling into the pattern of two old friends sharing tales. The experience of friendship with a man was a new one. Yet, as comfortable as she was, her deep attraction to him lurked constantly in the background to add a definite spiciness to their exchange.

The lodge was built around an old log cabin. Tastefully the proprietors had added rambling rooms and, in places, another story, to increase the size of the building. Behind the original cabin was a modern addition. For all its homey, countrified atmosphere, the lodge was luxurious and comfortable by any standards.

They were ushered to a table overlooking the valley below them. The evening had brought with it a scarlet sunset accenting the illusion that the mountains beyond the first ridge were melting into the sky. Lesley sat enthralled watching the sun disappear slowly. Finally she turned to see that Travis was watching her intently.

"I didn't grow up in this part of the world," she said softly, "but I knew I had come home when I first saw it."

"I thought you probably felt that way," he said, covering her hands with his. "The same thing happened to me."

Their waitress presented them with the menus and after a brief consultation, Travis ordered for them. The restaurant was well-known for its superb country cooking and Lesley and Travis succumbed to their desire to taste the home-cured country ham and the other trappings of a real country dinner. Left alone again, Travis took Lesley's hand and traced a pattern between the lines in her palm.

"Tell me about you. I keep asking, and you keep avoiding it. What terrible things are you hiding?" His blue eyes held a flicker of humor, but Lesley sensed the genuine interest.

What could she say? There were no details of her life that made for interesting listening. "One of three daughters, whiz kid in school, very shy, never married, and definitely not a hell-raiser." She looked at him seriously for a moment, and then the corners of her mouth turned up slowly. "While you were getting kicked out of school, I was buried up to my nose in the library. I decided somewhere along the way that being a scholar was going to be my salvation."

"From what?"

Lesley fidgeted in her seat a moment, wishing he would stop tormenting the sensitive skin of her palm. The gesture was too erotic to go well with country ham and innocent conversation.

"From what?"

"From real life, I guess." She pulled her hand away, turning his over to begin tracing patterns in it. "I think I've always been afraid to be anything, to do anything that wasn't related directly to my brains. Lately I've begun to wonder about that."

Travis was quiet, watching her finger move slowly over his palm. "You're a mystery to me. But I've always liked mysteries."

"That's a very interesting way to describe a not-very-interesting phenomenon, I'm afraid. There isn't anything too mysterious about me. It's just taking me longer to figure out who I am and what I want than it takes most people." Lesley squeezed Travis's hand before she picked up the glass of wine that he had ordered for her.

Travis leaned back casually in his seat. "Have you figured out what you want yet?"

Lesley looked carefully at the burgundy tablecloth, flicking an imaginary crumb off it. "It's becoming clearer to me." She tilted her head to see Travis watching her intently.

"When you figure it out, I hope I'll be the first to know." His eyes were inscrutable and Lesley felt compelled to question him.

"What about you? You're a mystery too. Sometimes you're the practical joker, all sly humor and innuendo. And then sometimes you're so serious and intense. Have you figured out who you are yet?" She watched his eyes light up slowly.

"I don't waste much time in introspection. I figure out what I want, and I go for it. It's always been pretty simple for me."

"What do you want, Travis?" The question hung in the air between them and Lesley made a conscious effort to keep breathing although the desire to hold her breath was unbearably strong. How had they gotten so serious?

The waitress arrived with platters of country ham, new potatoes accented with tiny fresh peas, steamed asparagus, piping hot biscuits and homemade preserves. Lesley relaxed as the arrival of the food served to make her question obsolete. Travis hadn't forgotten, however.

"Right now, I want to eat this scrumptious meal. And afterward?" He arched one eyebrow, lazily watching her. "After dinner I want to walk in the moonlight with you and straighten a few things out between us."

They finished the meal with coffee and rich apple pie made from Virginia apples stored over the winter. Travis told Lesley about the types of apples available locally, and the best methods of growing them. She was surprised to learn that there was an old apple orchard down the mountain from his house, and she felt a sharp thrill when he told her how he would teach her to make cider when the fall arrived.

The air was delightfully cool outside when Travis took her hand and led her to an open area behind the lodge. A gently sloping path lead down the mountainside to a clearing with large boulders and wooden benches set around the sides to sit on. "The owners hold church services down here in the summer, I'm told." Travis helped her step around a boulder. "Sitting with these mountains around you could make a believer out of anyone."

They found a bench to sit on and Travis moved close to Lesley, his leg pressed intimately against hers and his arm around her shoulders. They were quiet, enjoying the stillness interrupted only by the occasional whirring of insects and the far off bubbling sound of a spring. The air smelled of springtime merging gently with the faint tag of woodsmoke from a fireplace in the lodge.

Lesley slipped her arm around Travis's waist and leaned back a little, her head resting comfortably against his arm. "I'm waiting, Travis," she said at last.

"I understand that you spent an afternoon with Vivian a few weeks ago. I've been wondering if you were going to ask me to clarify anything that came up that day. Then I finally figured out that you would never bring this up yourself; you're much too private a person."

Lesley waited patiently. Travis was silent. Finally she prompted him. "I've just been waiting for you to tell me what you felt comfortable having me know."

Travis looked down and smiled at her, his teeth flashing white in the moonlight. "Do you ever make demands of people, Lesley?"

She thought seriously about the question. "Almost never."

"You settle for too little, but I guess I've told you that before. Anyway, I want to tell you about Vivian, and me and about T.J. But only if you want to hear it." The air seemed charged with suspense. Lesley wondered if she really wanted to hear what Travis was going to say. She had a feeling that it was important to him to tell her, but she was suddenly afraid that it might make a difference in their burgeoning relationship.

"Travis, I want to hear anything you want to tell me, but it can't make a difference, can it? I like Vivian and T.J. It's unusual that you have such a close relationship with her, but I'm a big girl. I can handle it." She had a sudden vision of Vivian, lovely and vibrant in the violet dress, and for a moment she wanted to call back her courageous words. Maybe she couldn't handle it after all.

Travis stood up and paced restlessly back and forth in front of the bench, coming to rest in front of her finally, with his foot propped beside her, his hand on his knee. "I met Viv when I was a sophomore in college. We were in an art class together. She was quite a catch back then, still would be I guess. Anyway, I dated her a few times and I decided that she was a perfect match...for my friend Joshua."

Lesley let the silence close in around them. She watched Travis as he remembered. Finally he continued with a sigh.

"Joshua and Vivian fell head over heels in love. I couldn't believe it. Joshua was the big stud on campus and suddenly he was completely wrapped around the finger of this beautiful redhead that I had introduced him to." Travis grinned, lost in the story of his past, his eyes gazing off into the darkness as if he were seeing ghosts.

"Were you jealous?"

"No, not of Joshua. I guess I was amazed. I had only heard about love; I'd never seen it up close. I remember thinking that I should be taking notes in case it ever happened to me." He shook his head slowly, shadows of pain flickering across his features.

"Vivian and Joshua were going to be married after graduation. I promised them I'd come back to be best man. I had dropped out of school by then to work on 'The Family Jones.' I went back instead for Joshua's funeral." Travis had worked the medallion loose from under his shirt and was pulling it back and forth as he talked. The sorrowful look on his face made Lesley want to reach out and hold him. Instead she waited quietly.

"Joshua was in love with Vivian and he was settling down, but he still had a wild streak. The night he was killed, Vivian had told him that she was pregnant with their child. Vivian told me later that Joshua was very excited. He went out after taking her home, to celebrate. I guess he had one too many and on the way home his car crashed and he was killed instantly."

The truth washed over Lesley like a mountain thunderstorm. She waited for Travis to go on, knowing what he would tell her. He held the medallion still for Lesley to see. "This was Joshua's St. Christopher's medal. His mother gave it to me at the funeral. I made a pledge to him that day, and this medal reminds me of that pledge."

"You married Vivian to give the baby a name, didn't you?" Lesley could no longer watch him search for the words. She felt as if her heart were being torn in two.

He nodded, looking straight at her for the first time. "T.J. is Joshua's son. Vivian and I were married a week after the funeral. When she told me about it, she had no place to go, no one to turn to. She had loved Joshua and wouldn't consider an abortion. She was going to go off somewhere by herself and have the baby until I convinced her that she owed it to the baby and to me to let me share in the experience." He smiled and for a moment Lesley knew he was very far away. "We were like two little kids. Both of us so completely torn up over Joshua. We clung together making plans for the baby, trying to create a marriage with nothing except our mutual love for Joshua and later of T.J."

Lesley shook her head slowly. "T.J. must have seemed like a real gift after all the sadness."

"T.J. was a miracle. Travis Joshua Hagen. I tried to get Vivian to just name him after Joshua, but she insisted on the T.J. part. She was right, of course. T.J. is as much my son as he is Joshua's. T.J. has no idea though. No one does except his grandparents and we only told them last year, although I knew they suspected."

Lesley thought about the implications of Travis telling her the story. She knew they weren't to be taken lightly. "You're going to tell T.J., aren't you?"

"When he's a little older. He knows all about Joshua. He's spent time with Joshua's parents and he likes them a lot. I think when the time comes, he'll be all right with it." Travis hesitated and then reached down to put his hand on

Lesley's hair. He trailed his long fingers down the side of her face and lifted her chin slightly to look into her eyes.

"Vivian and I wanted to make our marriage work. We never had the intention of just marrying so that T.J. would have a name. But being united because of the mutual love of a friend and of a child does not provide the essential ingredients to make a marriage succeed. God knows, we tried everything we knew to make a go of it. The simple truth was that we weren't in love. We couldn't make love grow. I care deeply about Vivian and she cares deeply for me, but the chemistry was never there for us. We finally decided to separate. We wanted to part friends and if we had waited much longer we wouldn't have."

Lesley reached up and brought Travis's hand to her face, feeling its hard strength against the softness of her cheek. "I'm very touched, Travis. I'm touched that you trusted me with this."

He sat down beside her again, turning her slightly to face him. "It's more than just trust, Lesley. I've met lots of people that I could trust with the story. But I wanted you to know. It was important that you understood how it is between Vivian and me."

"Why?" she asked in a small voice.

"Because I care about you," he said huskily as he pulled her close. "And I didn't want anything to stand between us."

The feel of his lips moving strong and hard against hers momentarily blocked out all thought, all concerns. The warmth of his arms wrapped tightly around her, the feel of his chest against the silk of her dress and the sweet taste of him drugged her senses. As his lips moved momentarily to her earlobe to nibble and torment, she sighed and whispered, "What you did for Vivian and for Joshua was beautiful, Travis. You're a very caring person."

Travis held her head against his chest and she heard the quick beating of his heart. "I didn't tell you the story so that you'd get some exaggerated picture of my virtue, Lesley. After the divorce I acted like a real Don Juan. I chased everything in skirts and made a habit of not spending more than one night in any bed. I was so disoriented from Joshua's death, T.J.'s birth and my failed marriage to Vivian that I think I made a vow never to take anything or anyone seriously again. It's taken me years, literally, to get over the trauma of those events."

"I can understand that," she consoled him.

"Be sure you don't settle for too little, Lesley. I'm still not sure I'm ready to make another commitment." His voice was low and his breath was warm against her forehead. Lesley thought about his words as he sat there holding her. She heard the pain echoing through the warning. Somehow it made her feel even closer to him. She knew instinctively that what Travis needed most of all was a bond, a loving relationship to ease the sorrow he had experienced. And throwing aside false modesty and shyness, she knew that she could give him what he needed. The thought gave her a glorious thrill. Travis Hagen needed her as surely as she needed him.

"Have I asked you for anything, Travis?" She pulled back slightly to search his face in the moonlight. "I'm not applying any pressure. It's coming from inside you. I'll take care of myself."

"There's something so vulnerable about you that I feel like I'm always going to want to protect you." His lips found hers again and they abandoned themselves to the sweetness of wild kisses and shared embraces.

The moon shone down with silvery patterns of light, faint tracings on the ground at their feet. Travis took Lesley's hand and they stood and walked a little farther down the path. Leaning against a wild apple tree fragrant with blossoms, she put her hands on his shoulders, absorbing the warmth and strength of him. His hands braced on the tree behind her, he gently kissed her nose, her eyelids, the soft skin of her neck.

"Lesley, I've told you about all my excesses. I guess I've sufficiently warned you off. How come we're still standing here?" His voice came from another place, another time. The words made no sense. She had made her decision, she had just neglected to tell him.

"Mmm...Travis," she said, wriggling slightly in pleasure at the feel of his tongue moving up to possess her ear. "If I weren't such a tremendously secure person, I'd think you were trying to get rid of me. However, my ego is so large that I can tend to overlook your maneuvers."

His laughter was deep and spontaneous. He pulled her up to stand against him, her cheek rubbing against the soft suede of his jacket. The rich smell of the leather and the feel of his hard body against hers combined to give Lesley a heady feeling, similar she thought to drinking champagne at a wedding. "You're not scared I'm going to hurt you?"

Standing in the moonlight with the most attractive man she had ever met was no time to be thinking about future pain. "Are you already planning to dump me, Travis? Is that what you're trying to tell me? Because you sure aren't acting like a man who's planning the end of a relationship."

Travis's arm tightened around her, and he lifted her head. "Actually, Lesley, I seem to be trying to avoid asking you if you'll spend the night with me tonight. I seem to be feeling shy and unsure of myself with you."

"Endearing qualities, Travis," she said, trying to sound nonchalant. His mouth met hers and she felt herself dissolving into him, merging with a fierceness and a desire to be his.

"Lesley, you're hedging," he murmured raggedly into her ear. "Where do we go from here?"

"Your place, or mine?" she whispered.

"Considering that they're both almost an hour away, how about here? The lodge has rooms as well as a restaurant."

Reality began to invade Lesley's thoughts. Travis wanted her now. Not later in the evening. Now. Now before she had time to figure out what she was doing, why she was doing it and the future ramifications of her actions. Now!

"Here, Travis?" She was playing for time and she knew it.

"Mmm...Yes, here." Whatever he was doing to her ear was affecting her brain, she decided. There must be a definite connection between the two organs. "Travis, I never thought about staying here tonight. And I, uh, don't seem capable of thinking about it now...,"

"Let's go. It's a wonderful place. The rooms have balconies overlooking the mountains. We can wake up tomorrow and have a romantic breakfast out on our own balcony. Or I'll bring you coffee in bed...or me."

Lesley felt a cold chill, almost but not quite wiping away the desire and longing she had felt in Travis's arms. She wanted him. She wanted him in the worst way. But she was sure it was going to spell the end of her relationship with him. Not because he said he wasn't ready for commitments, but because she was sure he would discover that she was terribly inadequate. "Travis." Her voice was anguished.

"I've really handled this badly, haven't I?" Travis moved away from her slightly, running his hand through his hair to bare his forehead for a split second. "You would be crazy to say yes. Here I've told you my bleeding heart story, then I've told you about my crazy behavior after the divorce. Follow it with a declaration of my reluctance for

commitments and end it with a proposition. You'd have to
be a masochist to say yes to me."

"Yes." The word was out of her mouth before she could
think about it. "Yes," she said again to be certain she had
heard herself right. She was surprised the second time too.

"Are you sure?"

"Do you always ask for an oath signed in blood, Travis?
For God's sake, yes. Let's get a room for the night. Let's
wake up together tomorrow. I'll decide about breakfast in
the morning."

She listened to the words, wondering who the strange
person speaking them was. Yes, she did want him. And she
did want to spend the night with him. But what kind of
humiliation was she letting herself in for? Compared to the
women he had known she was a babe in the woods, a
fumbling innocent who had only vague ideas about what
she had just agreed to. And yet, she was promising to give
herself to this man, to become a woman in his arms with
no assurance of a happily ever after. There could be only
one reason, and like an atomic explosion the truth descended upon her. She was in love with him!

Travis gathered her into his arms, kissing her hair, running his hands slowly, intimately down the length of her
spine, cupping her bottom with his fingers spread wide.
The ambivalence she was experiencing was either well
hidden or easy to ignore. He seemed extravagantly happy.
Lesley was terrified.

# Chapter Seven

Travis, I think we're making a mistake. I don't feel ready for this." Lesley paced back and forth. No, that definitely sounded too negative. She tried again. "Travis, I've really grown to care for you, but I'm not sure our timing is right for this step." It sounds like I'm rehearsing a dance routine, she groaned inwardly. "Travis, I'm scared to death!" Honest, forthright and altogether too revealing!

Lesley stood on the balcony of the room that Travis had taken for them and looked out into the darkness of the late evening. She was alone. Travis, able to sense her distraction, had tactfully left her there for a few minutes, telling her that he needed to get something out of his car. Practicing excuses to give him when he returned was only an exercise in futility. She knew that she did not have the courage to back down now.

Hugging herself unconsciously as a chilling breeze swept over the little balcony, she wished fervently that she could feel more at ease. There was nothing in the world that she wanted more than she wanted Travis at that moment. He'll be so turned off when he finds out what an inexperienced lover I am, she thought, he'll never have anything to do with me again. If she could only postpone this event a few weeks maybe she could read a manual, take a crash course from Masters and Johnson, or at least talk to her married sister.

"I can see you missed me; you need my arms around you." Lesley jumped as Travis encircled her waist with his arms. She reached down to cover his sure hands with her own trembling ones. "You know," he continued, "I like your shyness. I think it's one of the first things that attracted me. Modesty, shyness, vulnerability. They're qualities you don't usually associate with the modern woman." He slowly trailed his hands up her back to her shoulders, gently forcing her to turn around and face him. "I create characters with those qualities sometimes, but never any as wonderful as you."

"Travis…" she whispered, the warmth of his words making tiny fires to melt the icy fear around her heart. She reached up to stroke his face, her sensitive fingertips enjoying the faintly abrasive quality of his cheeks. She let her thumbs follow the strong jawline as she finally tangled her fingers in the soft hair at the nape of his neck, pulling his head down gently to kiss him.

"Not too shy, though. I'm glad." Travis made a low groaning sound as he wrapped his arms around her, pressing her body against his. His hands caressed her back with an insistent pressure. "I can feel so much more of you in this lovely dress, but not nearly enough. Come inside with me, Lesley."

"Uh, can't we enjoy this beautiful night a little longer?" Lesley asked in a voice that even to her own optimistic ears was no better than a strangled plea. Travis smiled knowingly and firmly guided her into their room.

"I have something for us." He walked to the bedside table and pulled a bottle of champagne out of the plastic ice bucket. "I brought this along because tonight was supposed to be a celebration of my return. Now we have something even better to celebrate." Pulling the Swiss army knife out of his pocket, he flipped out the corkscrew and deftly popped the cork. Pouring them each a tumbler full, he handed Lesley hers. "I propose a toast. No, better yet, I provide the champagne; you provide the toast." His eyes twinkled, causing Lesley's spine to stiffen slightly. He was teasing her.

"To Travis Hagen, Jr. A man who claims to be completely charming and lovable. May he have a chance to prove his words tonight." Travis choked on his first sip of champagne, snorting and sputtering between bursts of laughter. He sat down on the bed, looking up at Lesley with his eyes sparkling.

"It's got to be my turn now. A second toast. To Lesley Belmont, a woman who isn't sure what she wants. May she discover tonight that she can stop looking." Lesley groaned and moved slowly to sit beside Travis on the large bed. Their glasses clinked and Travis linked his arm through hers as they drank together.

"I thought they only did this at weddings," Lesley said as she slowly sipped the bubbly liquid, looking into Travis's eyes.

"It seemed appropriate."

Finally Travis broke the intimate contact to reach for the champagne, pouring Lesley another glass as he ignored her protests. "Lesley, you don't have to drive home. You don't have to get up early or go to work tomorrow. You don't have to keep your wits about you to fend me off. It's perfectly all right for you to have another."

She sat next to him, silently gulping her second glass. The champagne was trying to make inroads into her nervousness. She could feel the beginnings of something warm and tingly. Under the circumstances she decided Travis was right. "Travis," she said seriously, "are you trying to get me drunk so that it will be easier to seduce me?"

"Would it help?" He was looking down at her with his heart-wrenching, lopsided grin. "Let me know if it's working. I'd have to be blind not to see that you need something to help you relax."

Lesley shook her head mournfully. "I'm just fine, Travis." She continued to shake her head.

"Come here, love." He took her empty glass and set it down on the table. Propped against the pillows, he pulled her back to lean against him. "What is it? You can tell me. We'll straighten it out together."

She thought about what to say. "I'd like to be sophisticated and pretend I'm not anxious about what to expect. But I am. I guess that sounds pretty stupid in this day and time." She didn't add that she was terrified that Travis would reject her if he discovered that she was as much fun in bed as a Popsicle.

"We'll take it very easy, Lesley, my love."

The words and the new pet name sent more warmth to melt the ice inside her. What an incredibly special man Travis was. She brought his hands to her mouth, kissing the long powerful fingers, fingers that created small masterpieces every day, fingers that she knew could give her such pleasure as they touched her body.

"You're so lovely and so perfectly made. I consider this a rare privilege," Travis murmured. Lesley felt his warm breath on the back of her neck and then the caressing slide of his lips as he pressed warm, wet kisses under the springy tendrils that had escaped from the coil of hair.

"I hope you'll think so when we're finished," she said, without realizing how melancholy the words sounded.

"How could you have any doubts? You really have no idea of the effect you have on men, do you?" Travis's hands encircled her waist pulling her closer so that she had no choice but to lean fully against him. "Your perceptive abilities seem to go haywire when you turn them on yourself."

At that moment, Lesley's perceptive abilities were flying wild and free, not in the rational measured style she used in her research, but in a flood of feeling she couldn't deny. In fact, she couldn't be logical at all. She could only feel Travis's hands as they stroked her arms before coming to rest on her shoulders. And she could feel the seeds of regret sprouting to flourish inside her. Travis was going to be a magnificent lover. He was exquisitely gentle, concerned and reassuring, and his hands held terrifying magic. Soon he would coax from her the response he desired, and she would forget her worries to come alive in his arms.

Everything was perfect except that Travis didn't love her. He wanted her. It mystified Lesley but his desire was a tangible thing that she could not deny. And he needed her. Travis was reaching out for a deeper bond, more satisfying than the casual love affairs he had indulged in after his divorce. For almost any woman that would be enough. But for Lesley Belmont, who even took the comic strips seriously, there had to be more. If she understood one thing about herself, it was that her own intensity made this night together a very bad idea. She was a one-man woman. If her relationship with Travis ended abruptly, she would never find the courage to try again.

Travis began to knead the muscles carefully in the back of her neck and shoulders. He could gauge how tense she was by the unyielding feel of them. His fingers refused to take "no" for an answer, and he continued trying to massage away her stiffness. Satisfied when he began to feel a slight response and softening, he reached up to unpin the camellia. Laying it beside the bed, he took the hairpins and elastic band out of the thick shiny coil of hair.

"You don't want to go to bed with your hair like this; you'll sleep much better with it loose." Lesley felt her hair fall down her back like a heavy veil. Travis's fingers in the long thick mass sent shivering signals through her body as he smoothed out the tangles. The slow sensuous sound of the zipper being undone came next. Then there was the feeling of her hair and his hands against her back, and her dress being slipped down over her arms by slow inches.

"Your skin feels like satin," he murmured, his mouth descending to alternately taste and tantalize the nape of her neck and the smooth tender skin along her spine. His hands came around her to drift slowly over the rounded fullness of her breasts, stopping momentarily to unclasp her bra.

The room felt cool and Lesley shivered slightly. With a sense of panic she realized that the overhead light was still on. "Travis, umm...could you please turn off the light? I think I'd feel more romantic in the moonlight." She had committed herself to this night. She would not hurt him. Let him think her hesitation was due entirely to shyness.

He chuckled knowingly and slid off the bed to reach for the switch. The room was dark when he found his way back. "I love your modesty, but I'd love to look at that beautiful body of yours."

Lesley felt Travis in front of her, his hands on her shoulders. She sensed his lips close to hers and she leaned forward slightly to receive his kiss. Hungrily he pulled her closer, his hands roaming slowly to stroke her breasts under her silky slip. With what seemed like marked restraint he edged the straps of the slip and bra down over her arms as he softly caressed her, whispering reassuring words into the scented wealth of her hair. Tentatively she put her arms around him, experiencing the feel of his shirt against her naked breasts. Slowly she began to unbutton his shirt, baring his chest and running her hands through the crisply curling hair.

Travis finished removing his shirt quickly, pulling her against him again. She ran her hands down the length of his arms feeling the firm muscles, the inherent strength. Carefully he urged her back against the pillows, untying the belt of her dress and slipping it from underneath her. She was clad only in panties and the slip which hung around her slender waist in folds. With a spurt of incipient modesty, she held on to it as one small barrier between them. With good grace, Travis gave in, removing his slacks before coming to lie beside her.

In the darkness she could only dimly make out his body poised over hers. Lesley was torn with the desire to forget her fears and give herself wholeheartedly to the man she loved. Surely this couldn't be wrong. Surely she was strong enough to survive if it turned out to be a short-term romance.

Travis, propped on one elbow, was leaning over her, kissing her nose, her forehead. Teasingly he played with her breasts, stroking them with the whisper-soft movements of his hands. The sensation was like a sharp pain inside her, a longing for love that she knew would not be satisfied no matter how perfect the night was in other ways.... She stiffened sharply and Travis jerked his hand away from her as if he had been burned.

"Lesley, what is it?"

In answer she moved closer to him, determined to try, determined to make an attempt to satisfy him at least. "I'm sorry, Travis, I'm just a little anxious."

"More than a little," he said, reaching down to begin kissing her again. His hands on her body, his lips on hers, the sensations were glorious. She began to relax, to move slowly against the long hard length of his body. He felt so good, so like she had imagined he would. Even in her wildest fantasies this hadn't been how she had imagined it would be. The two of them together, loving each other with abandon.

But the words were wrong. What was happening was not love. She stiffened again, and Travis sighed.

"I can't stand much more of this, Lesley." He lay beside her for a moment and she could hear his breath coming in uneven gulps. Finally he sat up to turn on the lamp beside the bed. "I want to see your face while you tell me what keeps going wrong here." He ignored her protests as he clicked on the lamp. There was no answering flicker of light. With an oath that succinctly expressed all the frustration he was feeling, Travis reached behind the bed to check the socket. "Something is unplugged back here." He uttered another muffled oath as he leaned over to plug in the lamp.

The charge of power that surged through the electric cord did not result in light so that Travis could search for clues in Lesley's face. Instead the bed beneath them began to jolt and grind, almost catapulting Travis to the floor beside them. With a startled gasp, Lesley tried to sit up, succeeding momentarily as she grabbed Travis's hand. "It's an earthquake!" she cried.

"In Virginia?" Travis managed between the banging thuds of the bed.

"Tornado then!" Lesley grabbed the sheet and held on like a rodeo cowboy gripping a saddle horn. Certain that if she rolled to the floor she'd find it buckling beneath her, she held on for dear life.

A demonic sound thrilled through her, shattering Lesley's courage entirely until she realized that the noise was coming from the man next to her. Travis had collapsed in a fit of laughter. With no restraint at all, he moaned and tossed back and forth with the galloping rhythm of the bed. "Tornado!" he squeezed Lesley's hand between heady bursts of laughter. "My love, you're not Dorothy and you're not going to wake up in Oz. We're on a vibrating bed gone mad. I think it's possessed." Beside him Lesley bounced and jolted to the mad rhythm, the humor of the situation beginning to coax tentative giggles from her fear-clenched throat.

"I think they must have used this thing to prepare the astronauts for space travel," she gasped. Thrown up against Travis, she succeeded in holding tightly to him as they pitched and tossed over the surface of the bed. In a minute, both of them had reached the point of no return in their hysteria. The suddenness of the event and the tension preceding it combined to produce wave after wave of shared laughter. With a lack of inhibition she didn't even know was possible, Lesley laughed until tears coursed down her cheeks, nearly drowning the bouncing man beside her.

Finally, almost with regret, Travis rolled to the side of the bed, searching for the cord, between jolts, to pull the plug. The sudden cessation of movement left Lesley dizzy and disoriented. "Travis," she said, wiping the tears off her cheeks with a corner of the pillowcase, "come here. I need something firm to cling to."

In a moment he was in her arms, kissing her face, her neck, his hands entangling in her hair to trap her beneath him. Lesley's response was a surge of desire so powerful that she was sure it was a tornado inside her. "I want you, Travis Hagen," she said, her mouth seeking his. "I want you."

Her eyes had dropped shut as she savored his caresses and for a moment she ignored the absence of an answer. When the realization that Travis was no longer kissing her penetrated her dimmed senses, she opened her eyes to find him a distance away watching her thoughtfully. "I know you do."

Puzzled, she watched as he moved still farther away to lie on his side, not touching her at all except with his steady gaze. "What have I done wrong?" she asked, unconsciously gnawing on her lower lip. "Have you changed your mind about wanting me?"

Travis propped his head on his hand. "That would be impossible."

"Then why am I here and you over there?" She was bathed in disappointment, immersed in confusion. With trembling fingers she pulled the sheet up to her shoulders.

"Because I've just decided to stop being selfish." He sighed, wearily running a hand through his hair.

"I don't understand." Lesley flicked her heavy mane of hair over her shoulder, trying to hide her hurt expression in the dim light. Travis reached over and brushed the long hair away from her face.

"You're not ready for this. We both know it but I've been trying to ignore it all night. I wanted what you could give me so much that I was about to ignore what you need." His hand caressed her hair for a moment and then withdrew reluctantly.

"I was willing. I am willing."

"Part of you is, but the part inside that I can't touch isn't willing. You need more than I can give you tonight."

More vulnerable than she had ever been, Lesley shut her eyes to keep from crying. "I have never, in my entire life, known what to do or what to say around a man. But never, never did I think my clumsiness would come to this." Her words fell like frozen rain between them and just as she was reaching for the courage to sit up and find her discarded clothing, she felt Travis's arms close around her.

"Don't!" she snapped, trying to pull away.

"You're breaking my heart, love. Don't do this. Don't misinterpret everything I've said." Travis pulled her unwilling body against his, her head securely pinioned against his shoulder.

Scalding tears slid down Lesley's cheeks to baptize the bronzed skin of the man she loved. "I don't want your pity," she sniffed.

"Good. Because you can't have it."

"I don't want kindness either. I'm not a little girl who just dropped her ice-cream cone."

"Will you stop this, for God's sake?" Travis shook her against him roughly. "What you're going to get is my anger!"

The steely tones were a warning Lesley couldn't—even in her acute misery—ignore. "I want to go home."

"Not until we've talked about it."

She clamped her mouth shut, determined not to say another word that would expose more of herself to this man.

"First of all," Travis began, "I want you more now than I did when you were standing under the apple tree with blossoms floating around you."

Lesley sniffed in disbelief.

"Second, you are not clumsy, but you have another serious flaw, my love. You're so sure you're inept at dealing with men that everything that happens is colored by that perception."

"How can you say that," she snapped, forgetting momentarily that she hadn't planned to speak. "Look how tonight is turning out!"

"Tonight is turning out just as it should. Can you tell me honestly that you're ready to make love to me, that no matter what happens after tonight, you won't regret what we do in this room?" He tangled his fingers in her hair, pulling her head back so that she was forced to look at him. "If you can say that, then I'll spend the whole night making love to you, again and again, just as I really want to."

The words wouldn't come. Travis was right, and Lesley was defeated by his wisdom. "I'm sorry," she whispered, tears still streaking her cheeks. "I'm so very sorry."

"So am I." His finger trailed behind her last tear drop, coming to rest on her bottom lip. "I'm sorry I pushed you this far."

"I could have said 'no.' I should have."

"Yes, you should have. But I also know why you didn't."

Lesley tried to turn her head from his, but his fingers were still locked in her hair. "Please, Travis..."

"You're in love with me, aren't you?"

It was entirely absurd. Lesley Belmont in love with Travis Hagen. If she hadn't been so completely drained she would have dredged up a laugh at her own stupidity. "You won't take my body, so now you're trying for my soul," she said sadly. "They belong together, Travis. Please don't try to separate them."

"Don't run away from me, Lesley."

She shut her eyes briefly, weariness deadening all sensation. "After tonight, how will you bear to spend time with me, Travis? This is the end of the road for us."

"It's a turn in the road, a curve we can both maneuver. I'm not going to tell you I love you; I don't know exactly what I feel. But I do know I want to spend time with you, want to hold you in my arms when I can. I want whatever's between us to continue to grow, Lesley. Tonight's made me see that."

She was too weary to believe him, too tired to argue. "It's time to go home," she said.

"We're not going anywhere."

"I don't want to talk anymore," she said. "I just want to go home and get some sleep."

"It's entirely too late to drive these mountain roads. And I want to wake up with you tomorrow. Stay here with me. We'll go back in the morning."

Travis's suggestion was even more surprising than his earlier proposition had been. "What's the point?" she asked, her defenses gathered about her like the slip that she pulled up to cover her naked breasts.

"Very simple. I don't want to leave you tonight. We'll both get some sleep, and we can talk in the morning as we drive back home."

"Are you going to show me how platonic this relationship is by holding me in your arms all night? Will that prove something?" she asked warily.

"I'm going to sleep over there." Travis pointed to a single bed pushed against the far wall. "And when you're asleep I'm going to sneak lascivious glances at your lovely face and body and think lecherous thoughts."

Without conscious effort Lesley smiled a little and Travis's grin lit up the room. "I'm not sure what happened here tonight," she said cautiously, "but I do know I'm exhausted. Staying the night makes sense."

"There's only one thing."

Lesley lifted her eyes to meet his. "I don't think I can take too much more."

"Just don't do anything seductive in the next eight hours. My control is stretched about as far as it can go."

Somehow, the teasing words were just what she needed to hear. Travis still wanted her and he was letting her know it. She could almost believe that his reluctance to make love to her was to protect her from getting hurt. "What would it take?" she asked.

"Something major. Just don't look at me or walk within ten feet of my bed. Don't stretch or sigh or snore. Don't breathe."

"Thank you, Travis." Lifting on one elbow, she held the slip against her, planting a shy kiss on his willing mouth. "Now it's time for you to vacate my bed."

She watched as he stroked her cheek with unsteady fingers and sat up, swinging his long legs over the side of the bed. Picking up his slacks he rose and moved to the other side of the room. In a moment he was under the covers and Lesley was alone.

"Lesley?"

She sat up and peered across the expanse of darkness. "Yes?"

"Tonight hasn't been a disappointment for me. But someday soon, I want more."

As she lay in bed, her eyes began to shut slowly and she could feel the beginnings of peace radiating through her exhausted body. The picture of herself as a woman unable to handle a man in her life was fading away. She was who she was. And Travis still wanted her in spite of the problems between them. In spite of the fact that he knew she loved him.

Travis was not disappointed in her; he had not found her wanting. She thought about his last statement. Travis had no guile. Instinctively she realized that it would not even occur to him to make such a statement unless it were true.

Her sleepy brain tried to add up all the data it had received. Travis knew that she loved him. Travis understood now that for Lesley, making love was a commitment to love. Travis had told her that he still wanted her and that someday soon.... She drifted off to sleep wondering if the facts indicated that Travis might, just might, have been saying that it was possible he was falling in love with her too.

There was bright sunlight bouncing across her eyelids when Lesley awoke the next morning. Without opening her eyes, she stretched, contacting warm flesh with her wiggling fingers.

"Good Lord!" she said, sitting up in bed, blinking rapidly to obtain a clear picture of the charming male propped up in bed beside her. For a long moment she couldn't remember where she was or what had happened the night before.

"Your virtue is intact," Travis said helpfully. "Until an hour ago, I slept as lonely as a monk in the bed across the room."

"And what happened an hour ago?" she asked, pulling the sheet up under her arms.

"I woke up and decided to come watch you sleep."

Lesley blushed, aware of how vulnerable she must have appeared. "That's not fair!"

Travis shrugged. "You have the longest eyelashes. When you're asleep they almost touch your cheeks. And your skin is clear ivory against the pillowcase. You're so touchable I ache from restraining myself."

"Travis," she said, biting her lip. "About last night."

"Last night was last night. We can't pretend it didn't happen because it's made us set some new ground rules, but I want to continue seeing you."

She smiled shyly, opening her arms to him. In a moment the only thing between them was a sheer, peach-colored slip and some awkward memories. Travis covered her face with kisses, threading his fingers through her tumbled hair to slant her mouth to his. "Give me some time," he whispered against her lips. "Let me sort out my feelings. But stay with me while I do. Don't run from me."

Lesley was igniting with his touch, her heart pounding like a percussionist playing the "1812 Overture." "Travis, I won't run. Just try not to hurt me." His gentle touch and achingly tender mouth were the reassurance that she needed.

Later, when they could no longer avoid the realities of the need to return home, they reluctantly got up to shower and dress. Lesley, perching on the side of the bed to fasten her shoes, was almost jolted to the floor when Travis plugged the bed in for one more romp. They laughed appreciatively in memory of their encounter the night before.

Sipping cups of steaming coffee together on their balcony before they left, Travis put his arm around Lesley and held her for a moment. "I hate to leave, but if I stayed any longer, my good intentions would disappear like the scent of apple blossoms in a spring storm."

She smiled up at him, rubbing her head against the sleeve of his jacket in answer. From their vantage point on the balcony they could see the twisting, winding road leading up the mountain to the lodge. In the far distance Lesley noticed an old blue pickup moving slowly up the road. "Travis, do you see that truck?"

He squinted, searching the horizon before he shook his head. "My eyes must not be as good as yours. Why?"

"There's an old farmer that lives around here somewhere who drives a truck just like that one. He helped me change my tire on the way to see you the first time."

Travis stroked her arm. "And?"

"Well, I've seen him two or three times since then. It wouldn't be very interesting, except that this man looks like he poses for your drawings of Grandpa Silas Jones." She shrugged at his smile. "Really, he does. I've been meaning to ask you if you used a local person as a model."

"Don't forget, Lesley, my grandfather started this strip in New York City. Actually I always thought my grandfather looked like Grandpa Silas Jones."

"And you've never noticed the man I'm talking about?"

"Never." He shook his head.

"That's very odd. But I guess maybe you've just never run into him anywhere."

"Or my imagination isn't as good as yours."

"That's highly unlikely. After all you're the one who's making a fortune on your imagination. I'm just a poor working girl collecting facts."

"Tell me, my dear working girl," Travis said as he took her cup and set it next to his on the railing, "did you collect any facts last night?"

"Let me see." She pretended to think about his words. "I'm not sure. I'll have to go home and look carefully through the copious notes I took to see if I learned anything of value."

"Are you sure about that?" His arms came around her, his breath warm on her cheek. His lips moved to possess hers.

"Absolutely."

He kissed her again, his tongue gently opening her lips.

"Perhaps I learned a little," she gasped.

His hands moved along her back to pull her hard against him.

"Or a lot," she agreed with a moan.

"I'm sure of one thing," he whispered against her hair. "If I don't get you out of here in one minute, I'm going to have to pay for another night."

"Perhaps someday we can come back. Under different circumstances."

"I'd like that," he said huskily, "but for now, we need to get going. There's a little boy who is planning to spend the day at my house waiting for me back in Roanoke."

With regret they gathered up their few belongings and walked out into the Sunday morning sunshine. In the distance they could hear the sounds of hymns being sung from the direction of the clearing where they had strolled the night before.

"That explains the farmer's truck," Lesley said as she climbed into the car.

"The singing?"

"Yes, he must come here for Sunday services." A quick survey of the parking lot, however, showed no sign of the old blue Ford.

"I'm beginning to think this old fellow is a rival of mine," Travis said as he got into the driver's seat.

"If he were just forty years younger," Lesley said with a playful shake of her head.

"Yes?" Travis lifted one eyebrow to try and offset the lopsided smile. "If he were forty years younger what would you do?"

"I'd consider myself very lucky to have two such fascinating men in my life," she said, sliding across the seat to sit closer to him. "Who could ask for anything more?"

# Chapter Eight

I was in the bathroom getting ready for work when I heard the doorbell ring and a voice yell 'U.P.S. man.'"

Sylvia finished the doughnut she was eating, sucking the syrupy sugar glaze off her fingers as she listened to Lesley's story. "And?"

"And I went to the door, threw my arms open wide, and puckered up for a big kiss."

Sylvia put her chin on her hands and wore her most expectant look. "So then what happened? Was he surprised to see you like that?"

"Oh, he was very surprised, all right. The only problem was that it really was the U.P.S. man this morning, not Travis. My birthday is this month and my sister in New York sent me a present. I think the poor delivery man thought I had flipped."

Sylvia sat back in her chair and laughed until tears fell down her cheeks. "That's great. I love it."

Lesley laughed too. It was Monday morning, she was in love, and it felt good to be alive. "I signed the slip, took the package and managed to keep my composure in place. What a way to start a week."

"His or yours?" They both laughed appreciatively. Sylvia wiped her eyes and called to Lesley who had gathered a pile of papers and was heading toward the door. "You look terrific this morning. I like that skirt and blouse on you. It does nice things for your figure."

Lesley looked down at the orange silk blouse and camel skirt. She did look nice, so nice in fact that she had looked in the mirror that morning and failed to recognize the radiant young woman staring back at her. There was a glow that seemed to come from deep inside that had nothing to do with makeup or color or style of clothing. It was love, plain and simple. She had fallen in love with a wonderful man, and she was becoming more sure by the moment that eventually that love would be returned.

Still, the outside accessories didn't hurt. She had decided to stop in Roanoke that day on her way back from the library to have her hair styled. It was the one change she had avoided because it seemed so permanent, so final. Today she didn't care. "Thanks. By the way, where's Gerald?" she asked, suddenly realizing that there had been no sneering face to greet Lesley that morning, no one to attempt to take the sparkle from her eyes.

"He called in sick." Sylvia's voice was level, without her usual humorous twinge. "You know, I think he's coming to a fork in his road. He's not going to be able to continue living the way he is and keep this job."

"Do I hear concern in your voice?" Lesley's question precipitated a faint pink blush that coordinated nicely with Sylvia's gray hair.

"Don't you have to be somewhere now, dear?" the older woman answered.

Lesley smiled. "I'll be at the Roanoke library most of the day. See you tomorrow."

The research went quickly. Lesley looked at what seemed like miles of microfilm, occasionally making copies of significant strips, usually just taking notes. With a short break for coffee and a turkey sandwich at a drugstore near the colorful Roanoke farmer's market, she was done at two, just in time for her appointment with the hairstylist that Vivian had recommended.

The shop was bright with mirrors and forests of hanging plants. Instead of outdated celebrity magazines and rock and roll to entertain waiting customers, there were *National Geographic* and the daily *New York Times*. Piped in as background music was a classical radio station. Lesley felt instantly at home.

When it came time for her turn in the stylist's chair, she panicked, almost turning to leave. Sensing her distress Mister John firmly steered her to his cubicle, asking questions about her job and discussing books that they had both read. She cringed as she watched layer after layer of hair disappear, but he promised her that it would not be short when he was done. Just at the point where she was sure he had lied to her, he stopped snipping.

Rinsing the finished product with henna, he combed the newly tamed layers of wet hair, pushing them into waves as he dried her hair with a blower. "See, there will be very little you'll have to do to it." When her hair was all dry and curling softly around her shoulders Lesley looked at herself with amazement.

"I think I've just reached the 'after' stage of a before and after series," she said. Her hair waved and tumbled to her shoulders with controlled abandon. The gleaming, silky chestnut locks framed her face, emphasizing her classic features. She looked carefully to see if she could find anything out of place. She couldn't. No modeling agency was going to search for her; no talent scout would ever stop her at a soda fountain; no strange man was going to put his cloak over a puddle for her to walk on, but it didn't matter. She was pretty. She never had to think of herself as plain or unattractive again. "I don't know if I can cope with the difference," she said happily, "but I'm sure going to have fun trying."

Outside the stylist's salon, Lesley debated what to do. It was only three-thirty and she had time to waste if she wanted to. On an impulse she decided to go to The Rainbow Connection to show Vivian and GeorgeAnn the changes she had made. They would definitely be pleased.

Parking the little Pinto in the sprawling lot she wandered through the mall for a few minutes before turning in at the door of Vivian's salon. "Hello, GeorgeAnn, remember me?"

GeorgeAnn looked up and smiled in delight. "Lesley, you look fantastic. Let me get Vivian." She walked into the back of the shop, leaving Lesley alone to wander around the waiting room, examining color charts on the wall. The outside door tinkled as someone entered and a big, warm hand settled on her shoulder, turning her slightly to face its owner.

"I almost didn't recognize you. What have you done to yourself?" Travis was watching her steadily, a faint smile on his face. For a moment Lesley couldn't tell if he approved of the "new her," or not.

"Travis," she said shyly. "I didn't expect to find you here."

"I wanted to work out details with Vivian about next weekend." He saw the confusion in Lesley's face and chuckled. "I wanted to see if she would keep T.J. for me. I have plans I'd like to explore with a certain young woman. Much as I love T.J., I really don't want to share this particular woman with an eleven-year-old boy so soon in our relationship. Now, what have you done?''

"I had my hair cut." Hating herself for needing to soothe her insecurities, she went on. "What do you think?''

Travis examined her carefully, seeming to enjoy the embarrassment his slow assessment was causing. "You're too pretty. I'm not crazy about having to fight off lots of other men. But I guess I can cope." He grinned broadly at her obvious relief, then chided her gently. "Just don't go cutting anymore off. I enjoy running my fingers through it.''

"That's why I left it long," she said softly. "For you.''

Travis bent to kiss her, his hands coming up to tangle gently in the silky hair, his thumbs caressing the downy soft skin over her cheekbones. "There's a certain glow about you that doesn't have anything to do with that new hairstyle." He laughed as her cheeks flushed delicately. "Come home with me. Spend the rest of the day with me.''

Caution pounded through her head, but desire and delightful expectancy poured through her veins. "I'll come.''

"We can leave now. I'll call Vivian later.''

"Are you sure? Vivian— Oh, Travis," Lesley said as she turned to look behind the counter, "GeorgeAnn went to get…''

"Hello," Vivian stood in the doorway beaming at the two of them. "Don't let me interrupt anything.''

Lesley felt a wave to heat suffusing her as Travis's grip relaxed. "Hello, Viv," he said, pulling Lesley to stand in the crook of his arm. "How are you? How's the baseball star?''

Vivian's delicate face held a smile almost too big for it. "We're both fine, thank you. T.J. had a good time at your place yesterday." She looked benignly at the two of them. "But I think that he's going to be way too busy this weekend to come spend time with you. Would you mind too much if we skipped this once? School will be out in a few weeks and you can see him all you want then."

"I guess I can manage. I'll pick him up Wednesday after school and he can spend the night if that's all right." Travis didn't bother to hide his delight at Vivian's perception.

"Fine." She looked at Lesley appraisingly. "If you ever need a job, there's a standing invitation to join my staff. We could use another beautiful Autumn."

The tactful compliment filled Lesley with a warm glow. Vivian would not be any more direct about the changes that she had helped bring about, but her approval was obvious. Again, Lesley marveled at Vivian's unique ability to be so genuinely diplomatic in every situation.

"Thank you." Lesley's gratitude was apparent in her smile, and Vivian beamed back.

"Well, I've got to get back to a customer. Take care, you two." She disappeared through the door.

In the parking lot, Lesley and Travis made arrangements to meet at his house, and she watched as the big silver station wagon pulled into the street. The lingering doubts she had about Travis's continued interest disappeared as the car was lost to sight. His signals were clear. There was a connection growing between them that had even survived the painfully abortive night at the lodge. Travis was making room for her in his life, and Lesley hoped that soon he would find there was also room in his heart.

Travis and Lesley made a simple supper of cheese and fruit and ate it on the kitchen deck, looking out over the mountains surrounding them. Travis insisted on feeding Lesley grapes one by one, Roman style. She dribbled wine down his chin while trying to pour it slowly into his waiting mouth. In recompense she licked every drop, savoring the taste of him through the good Burgundy.

"I'll bet you do this as often as you can," she murmured in contentment, snuggled in his arms after the food was all gone.

"Oh, every night I'm out here with someone, sitting just like this," he teased.

She buried her face in his shirt and laughed self-consciously. "You know that's not what I meant. I meant you must eat out here every chance you get."

"You're right. The house seems too big, too empty. I'm either out here or in my studio most of the time."

"I can't believe you get lonely," she said wistfully, realizing too late the implications of her statement.

"While we're trying so hard not to be on the subject," Travis said, stroking her hair, "I ought to tell you that although I was very, shall we say, active after my divorce, I haven't had anyone here in a long time."

"Travis, don't! You don't have to explain anything," Lesley agonized.

"Hush, my love. I want to tell you. I was completely faithful to Vivian while we were married. But our marriage quickly became a marriage in name only. I couldn't touch her without seeing Joshua and she couldn't respond because of her own feelings of grief and guilt. We both realized right away that it wasn't going to work out for us."

"Travis, please."

"Hush." His voice was a command. "After the divorce, I quite frankly felt like a dam had burst. I was so emotionally raw that I seemed to need constant solace with no commitments. But that got old very fast, and I decided to get off the treadmill. Vivian had visited a friend here and investigated the possibilities for opening her business. When she mentioned moving to Roanoke I came to sightsee and fell in love with this country. I decided that I wanted to own a part of it so I moved here, bought this land and decided to build this house. It was the first stable, mature thing I had done since I had the sense to end my marriage."

Lesley lay still in his arms, feeling the tension that had temporarily taken hold of him begin to ease. "So you built this huge, wonderful house and came to live here."

"Yes. When I asked the architect to design it, I asked for a small compact space, big enough for a bachelor with a visiting son. When I looked at the design, I knew it was wrong. I realized that I didn't always want to live that way. I wanted a real home, and someday a family besides T.J. I wanted a wife and I wanted more children. And that's why this house is so big...and so empty."

Travis's honesty filled Lesley with warmth, and with hope. There was no reason for him to share this with her unless he was trying to tell her something more important. She waited.

"I had the house built, but I don't seem to be able to really live in it by myself. I've never done any decorating, any landscaping. I think I've just been waiting for the right moment, the right help." He turned her face up to his, separating her from the safety of his chest.

"I'm sorry you thought I was prying," she said, looking into the eyes that rivaled a summer sky. "You didn't have to explain yourself to me. I'm not making any judgments."

"I didn't think you were. But I wanted to tell you anyway."

"I'm glad you did then."

"One more confession. Then you'll know everything there is to know about me."

"You're going to tell me your shoe size?" Lesley raised her head slightly to kiss him. "In case I ever want to buy you slippers?"

"No, I'm going to tell you that I was lying the other night when I said I wasn't looking for a commitment. I guess I am."

"Travis, you don't have to...I didn't expect..." She let her head fall back to his chest, her eyes shutting briefly.

"I've already figured out that you expect nothing from me. I'm here to tell you to raise your expectations, my love." He gently kissed her eyelids, his lips traveling downward to claim hers in a kiss that brooked no resistance. "And my shoe size is ten and a half. You can buy me a pipe to go with the slippers."

Silently they both absorbed the new closeness that was developing so rapidly. Their relationship seemed to be careening toward a new destination, a mysterious place that neither of them had ever been and weren't sure they would recognize if they got there. The only thing that Lesley was sure of was that if they continued in the direction they were heading, they would arrive together.

Later, wearing an old college sweatshirt of Travis's and a pair of worn jeans that she had to roll up and secure with a belt buckled in a hand-punched notch, Lesley followed Travis down an overgrown path leading to the apple orchard that he had told her about. They moved slowly, stopping to search for the wildflowers covered by the bushy undergrowth. The orchard was filled with old gnarled trees that were still in bloom, although the ground underneath them was a carpet of fallen blossoms.

"Soon these old trees will bear fruit again. Some of the varieties aren't even readily available anymore. And they're so good. That's progress, I guess." Travis took Lesley's hand and they wandered through the acre of trees, examining them for signs of the fruit that would soon be evident.

A weather-beaten shed revealed an old hand-cranked apple cider press. To her delight Travis showed Lesley the mechanics of pressing cider.

"I always buy fresh cider when I see it at the roadside stands outside of Christiansburg," she told him, her eyes sparkling with anticipation. "I'll bet it's even better if you drink it as soon as you make it."

"I'll show you come fall. We'll have a party and everyone can come down here with us." He gathered her close to him. "Or maybe we'll just come down here by ourselves. There aren't any snakes to worry about in the fall. And I can think of a few things I'd like to do besides make cider."

They climbed back up the mountain before it got too dark to see the path and sat quietly on the deck again. There seemed to be no need to say anything. Lesley lounged in Travis's arms with a contentment she had never before felt.

Finally Travis broke the silence. "This probably sounds like a strange question, but do you read my comic strip?"

Lesley laughed softly. "I'm hooked on it. Completely. It's gotten to be the first thing I do in the morning."

"Mmm...We'll have to change that, won't we?" he said as he nuzzled the nape of her neck.

"I can't imagine what you mean," she sighed innocently, a teasing note in her voice.

"Really?" he said. "Have you been following my new episode?"

"Uh-huh. I'm anxiously waiting for the story to develop, just like half of America is."

"Not quite half, my love. But anyway, do you have any idea what's going to happen next?"

Shaking her head, she began to run her hands down the muscular jean-clad thighs stretched out around her. The slight roughness of the denim taut against his skin was a pleasure to stroke. "Something to do with Bubba, I think. The story seems to be focusing on him."

"Very perceptive. Your research has given you profound insights," he teased, immediately following it with a yelp of pain. "Pinch me again, and you'll be sorry," he warned.

"I'm properly threatened," she said mildly, not in the least bit alarmed.

"Anyway, I just wanted to tell you that the story really gets going tomorrow. After breakfast I'm going to take you to the studio and show you the whole episode. You can see the next six-weeks' worth that way."

"Breakfast? I'm a working girl, remember? I'll be at my desk tomorrow morning."

"Come back up early and eat with me. I don't want to waste the evening on anything serious, but I do want to discuss the strip with you. Consider it part of your job."

"But then you'll spoil it for me. What will I have to look forward to every morning?"

"Me." He yelped again. "Remember what I said about pinching me?" His hands crossed in front of her creeping slowly underneath the sweatshirt. "Now I'm going to make you sorry you pinched me again."

"I'm shaking with terror," she said with a happy sigh. "If this is punishment, I'd love to see what a reward is like."

Travis's hands lightly caressed the delicate skin, his fingers fluttering casually over her hardening nipples under the thin bra. "I just want you to see them with me so I can explain them to you."

"See what?" she asked in a glorious daze.

"The comic strips, Lesley. Concentrate now. Tomorrow we are going to look at the new episode of my comic strip together." His voice was husky with repressed laughter and something much more exciting.

"I'll try to concentrate. I definitely heard you say strip." She felt his hand unhook her bra to begin a slow assault on her sanity.

"To think that you would turn into such a wanton, young lady. It's a good thing I have incredible self-control."

"Everything about you is incredible, Travis," she said, her voice unconsciously low and seductive. "Absolutely incredible."

Later they lounged on mattresses dragged down from the lounge chairs, their bodies a kiss apart in the glowing moonlight. Lesley traced patterns in the curly brown hair covering Travis's bared chest. "Isn't it nice," she whispered, as if afraid to break the spell. "Isn't it nice that this deck stays firmly planted on the ground where it belongs and doesn't vibrate or rock?"

A low chuckle rumbled through Travis's chest. "You definitely don't need the diversion anymore, my love."

Lesley lifted her head and looked at him with suspicion. "Just what does that mean?"

"Well, I don't have to plug in an out-of-order vibrating bed to loosen you up anymore." He watched her eyes widen.

"You mean you did it on purpose? You knew?" Her tone was menacing.

"Well, when I went to reserve the room, I was warned about it. Forgive me, but it did seem to be just the thing to make you forget how frightened you were." He caught her arms. "You've got to admit that it worked. Almost too well."

She collapsed against him, her head lying on the cushion of the mat of hair on his chest. "Is our relationship going to be one practical joke after another?"

"Mmm...our relationship is no joke, my love." His hands ran down the denim-clad thigh pressed against his. "No joke at all."

Lesley wondered why she needed anything else from Travis. Surely any other woman would be satisfied with what he had just said. Why did she have to hear three short words before she felt sure enough to give herself to this man? About to voice her thoughts, Lesley felt Travis's finger on her lips.

"It's getting late. If you stay here any longer, I won't let you go."

"I'm not sure I want to."

"And you're not sure you don't." He kissed her on the forehead and then pushed her gently away. "Until you are sure, it's better that you leave. Come back tomorrow when you're not bewitched by the moonlight, and we'll talk then."

At her car door, Travis convinced Lesley with one thorough kiss to make the trip back up the mountain the next morning. "I'll have to come early," she warned as she reluctantly turned away to get into the car.

"Wake me up; I'll leave the front door unlocked."

Driving over the curving, moonlight-flooded roads, Lesley wished that she was brave enough to pull into one of the sloping driveways and turn her car around. Travis would be surprised to see her again, but she knew he would also be pleased. It would be an act of commitment, a symbol of the unspoken bond that was developing between them. But one driveway looked too steep, one too narrow, and before Lesley could find the perfect place to turn her car around, she was back in Christiansburg, wondering how she could be such a fool.

The sun had just peeked over the eastern mountain ridge when Lesley pulled into Travis's driveway. When she had told Travis that she would be early, she had not meant this ungodly hour, but after a long restless night, she had finally given up the pretense of sleep and had risen with the earliest birds. Even after an inordinately long shower and session at the closet trying to decide what to wear, she was still ready to go when the rest of the world was sleeping soundly.

Travis was one of those people. When Lesley tiptoed quietly into his house, there were no noises audible. The path to Travis's bedroom was firmly imprinted in her mind, and she followed it, peeking through the open door to find him sprawled across the water bed, sound asleep.

He looked so peaceful, such a glorious combination of dreaming little boy and heart-wrenching man that she couldn't bear to wake him up. Lesley stood for long moments watching him sleep, wishing that she were tucked underneath the arm that cradled his pillow. Turning finally, she went back through the house.

Debating whether to cook breakfast or go for an early morning walk, she decided to hike up the gravel driveway to the mailbox where Travis probably had his morning paper waiting for him. The early morning air was clear and cool with no hint of the warm afternoon that would follow. Walking silently along the driveway Lesley encountered a family of quail out for their morning constitutional. The mother quail was so anxious to get her babies out of Lesley's way that she pushed and prodded them, their little bodies tumbling head over feathers with the effort to move quickly enough. Lesley laughed in delight, the sound bounding back to her in miniature echoes.

The paper was waiting for her inside the oversized mailbox and she tucked it carelessly under her arm as she started back down the driveway. The colors and smells of a late spring morning assailed all her senses. She wanted to dance, sing and shout her happiness. Instead she walked leisurely along, breathing the pungent air as she feasted her eyes on the dew-washed countryside.

Lesley half expected to find Travis awake and waiting for her, but when she heard no noise from the house upon her return, she curled up in a lounge chair on the deck off the living room and admired the mountains as she sat quietly for a few minutes before opening the paper.

The headlines were dreary, as usual. The morning was too bright to be ruined that way, she decided, flicking through the city section and the women's pages until she reached the comic page. Her eyes sought "The Family Jones" with latent curiosity. Travis had made the day's strip sound important, and she wanted to be able to make an intelligent comment about it when they talked.

Expecting to be entertained, Lesley stared at the black and white drawings a full minute before she realized the impact of what she was seeing. Cold chills ripped through her as she recognized the caricature in the second frame. The character's name might be Lily, but the severe bun, the glasses and the outdated clothing made it perfectly apparent who Travis had had in mind when he'd drawn the strip. The paper drifted to the deck, a hapless sacrifice to Lesley's suspicions.

Consumed by humiliation, she stood grinding the comics with the heel of her shoe. There were only four frames on the page. What could she tell from four frames? There must be a horrible mistake, a misunderstanding. Feverishly she wracked her brain for a way to clarify what she had seen. Looking out over the deck she caught a glimpse of Travis's studio set back from the house. Quickly she descended the stairs, her heel catching on a loose board and nearly tripping her. Heedlessly she continued down the steps until she was on the ground, almost running toward the little building.

The door was locked, but Lesley knew that Travis kept the key hidden under a stone beside the door. She had teased him about it once because the hiding place was so obvious. With uncoordinated fingers she grappled with the key and opened the door, pausing only to close it behind her. Familiar with Travis's filing system from her days of research there, she pulled out the drawer with copies of his most recent strips. The folders were neatly marked, and she sat down on the couch with trembling hands to read the series.

In a minute she knew that her worst fears were a reality. Tears streamed down her face as she poured over several weeks of the strip. Lily, obviously a caricature of Lesley, was shown as a homely spinster whom Bubba Jones kept running into in the course of his job behind the counter at the general store. Lesley groaned in tearful agony at the awkwardness, the painful shyness of the cartoon character. Bubba was a womanizer, a free spirit clothed in overalls but with the wit and determination of any city slicker. Lily seemed to have no purpose other than to be a target for laughter.

The pain was too much to bear. Lesley slammed the folder shut and dropped it on the floor at her feet. One coherent thought rang through her brain. She had to get out of there and she had to do it quickly. All her life she had expended a tremendous amount of energy to keep herself from being hurt. Her defenses had been lowered with the force of Travis's persistence, and she had willingly opened herself up to the most painful encounter of her entire life.

Travis had been laughing at her all the time. From the beginning he had humiliated her; he had looked on her as material for his comic strip. He had patronized her, pretended to be attracted to her, pretended to care for her. He had gotten her into his life and almost into his bed. She wondered what twinge of conscience had kept him from carrying out that part of the plan. Or perhaps it hadn't been conscience at all, just distaste for the idea. What a laugh he must have been having the whole time. Travis, the consummate practical joker.

Flinging the door open, Lesley started down the path from the studio, carefully skirting the house. With an almost childlike terror of running into Travis, she walked under the shade of the big maple and poplar trees rimming the yard. In the driveway, she fumbled with her keys, flooding the engine in her anxiety. Refusing to wait the necessary minutes, she tried again and finally the engine caught with a cough and a sputter.

Lesley was almost out of the driveway before she noticed the old blue pickup parked almost in front of the entrance to the road. Slamming on the brakes, she leaned her head out the window to snap at the old man. He gave her a penetrating glance, shaking his head slowly, his face troubled. Ignoring him, she jammed down the gas pedal, making a wide sweep around his truck, and shot out into the road.

She covered the miles to Christiansburg quickly. The tears of anguish had long since dried on her cheeks. They were replaced with a burning anger and a sense of betrayal that was like a fire inside her. That she could ever have let something like this happen was unforgivable. She had walked into the trap blindly, foolishly. Travis Hagen was no different from the man she had first imagined him to be. He was an insensitive, cruel man who got his kicks out of humiliating others. He had gotten his revenge for the way that he had been treated by Gerald, and in his eyes, by Gerald's accomplice, Lesley Belmont. Travis Hagen had played the best practical joke of all time.

The little tan Pinto would announce that she was home to anyone who cared enough to find out, so when Lesley reached her block after the long miserable trip, she circled the area, finally deciding to park behind an apartment complex several doors from her own dwelling. Furtively she scanned the street to be sure that Travis was not waiting for her. Although she had no reason to think that he might follow her, she was apprehensive that he might want to see her again, perhaps to confront her with the truth or even a twisted apology. And that was one satisfaction that she could still withhold.

Inside the little apartment Lesley drew the heavy curtains and left the lights off. She pulled out her set of suitcases and randomly began to throw her clothes into them. Working as quickly as she could in the dim light of the tiny rooms, she was almost finished when a loud pounding began on her front door.

"Lesley, open this door!" The command was unmistakably issued in Travis's voice. Lesley sat on the bed not making a sound, not taking a breath. The pounding continued and she covered her ears. The sound had body and substance and it felt as though it was piercing her brain.

Suddenly there was silence. Lesley didn't move; she was frightened that Travis might be trying to trick her into giving herself away. She imagined him outside the door with his ear pressed to it, listening. The banging began again.

"Lesley, if you're in there, for God's sake open this door." His voice was angry, but there was a helpless quality about it that gave her a momentary twinge. Quickly she pushed the thought away. Poor, poor Travis. He was being cheated out of the chance to see her in her misery. Her spine stiffened imperceptibly. He would never have that satisfaction.

Finally the pounding ceased. Footsteps sounded, heading down the steps in a stampede. Taking a deep breath, she moved silently to the door, standing with her ear to it, listening. There were no sounds in the hall. She walked softly to the living-room window, pulling the curtains apart a scant half-inch to peer out. Her heart wrenched as she saw Travis get into the jeep, pull out of his parking space and tear down the street.

On wobbly legs she walked back into the bedroom and finished packing. She knew that she had to get out of the apartment immediately. Travis would be back. He was perfectly capable of battering down her front door, and he might very well try it next time. She had no intention of staying around to find out if he would. Taking the back fire escape, she carried the suitcases to her car, one by one, breathing heavily toward the end with the exertion. She made one last trip to be certain that everything was locked and in order, stopping momentarily to splash water over her plants.

A stop by the bank, a fill-up at a gas station, and she was out on the highway heading for North Carolina. During the trip from Travis's to Christiansburg, she had come to the conclusion that she must get out of town. There was nowhere to go except home to North Carolina to see her parents. She knew that she would be welcomed with open arms, and she knew that the diversions there would be soothing to her ragged nerves. Completely desolate, her heart literally feeling as though it had broken, she felt a need for the comfort and reassurance that her family would provide.

And her home town of Clifton had one other strength to recommend it. It did not carry "The Family Jones" in the local paper. Clifton only had a weekly paper, and the big city paper that was also available did not, to Lesley's knowledge, carry the comic strip. She would not have to face herself in the papers every day.

An hour down the road she pulled into a chain restaurant. The gigantic statue of a young boy and a hamburger alerted her to the fact that she could get a quick, if uninspired, meal, find clean rest room facilities, and use the telephone.

She ordered the breakfast special and forced herself to eat, but when she was finished she could not have answered one question about the meal. The waitress was friendly, perhaps sensing her desolation, and tried to engage her in conversation, but Lesley was incapable of a response.

She paid for her breakfast, changing a five-dollar bill for the phone, and placed a call to Christiansburg. Sylvia's cheerful voice answered on the first ring. With a voice that sounded like it was coming from a casket, Lesley explained that she was quitting her job, and asked Sylvia to please stop in occasionally and water the plants in her apartment. Lesley could only give exhausted, noncommittal replies to Sylvia's startled questions. Finally, swearing Sylvia to total secrecy as to her whereabouts, she asked her to forward her paycheck to her parents' home.

The next voice on the line was Gerald's. Lesley flinched at the necessity for this confrontation on top of the other emotional storms of the morning. As simply and unemotionally as she could, she told him that she was resigning.

"Did your lover boy cartoonist have anything to do with this sudden decision?" Gerald's voice was a sneer, and Lesley felt her legs beginning to buckle beneath her. She leaned against the wall, her head bent slightly.

"I'm not giving you any reasons, Gerald. I'm just quitting." In spite of herself, Lesley's voice shook with raw emotion.

"Hagen was here today looking for you. He seems to think that you misunderstood something." Lesley had a vision of Travis discussing her with Gerald. Two of a kind, she thought. They'll make great buddies.

Gerald's voice took on a wheedling quality. "Come back, Lesley. Now that this episode with Hagen has ended, we can start over again. It doesn't matter to me if the man made a fool out of you."

Through the haze of exhaustion and depression that was threatening to overwhelm her, Gerald's words hit like a lightning bolt. Nauseated by his suggestion, she almost screamed into the phone. "Gerald, I don't want you. Do you hear? You're a sick man and you need help. You're living in an alcoholic fantasy world. Straighten yourself out, Gerald, before it's too late." Lesley hung up the phone before the sobs that were threatening to engulf her began.

With a gulp and a small cry she pushed the door of the rest room open, giving way to her helpless agony only when she was certain that she was completely alone. Sob after sob shook her until there were no other sobs remaining. Finally she took a deep breath and splashed handfuls of icy water on her face and neck. Running a brush through the tangled hair she saw that she looked like a shadow. But there was a glint in her eye that the tears had not washed away. She was going to make it. The tearing agony inside her would be there for a long time, but one day it would lessen. Come hell or high water she would not let Travis Hagen ruin her life. Straightening her shoulders Lesley left the restaurant to continue her lonely journey.

## Chapter Nine

Nothing could be finer than to be in Carolina in the mor...or...or...ning.'' Lesley stopped in the middle of the sidewalk, shading her eyes from the blazing sun. That song, that sound had come from her own throat. The realization numbed her with surprise. She walked over to the shade of an awning stretched over the window of the town's only jewelry store and pretended to examine the display of necklaces and rings set with rubies, sapphires, and diamonds. The fourth of July holiday was only a week away, and every store in the little town was preparing for it. In the middle of the window was a red, white and blue music box with a little boy playing a drum.

Standing there looking at the traditional decorations, the comfortingly familiar shops, Lesley could almost pretend that she had never left Clifton at all. The song she had been singing softly was one that she and her sisters had loved to compose obscene lyrics to in the privacy of their

bedroom. That she could forget her problems long enough
to find herself singing it was a step in the right direction.

Walking down the street, she ducked into the five-and-
ten to pick up a few items her mother had insisted she
couldn't live without. Mrs. Belmont was always making up
errands for Lesley to do. "You need to get out of the house
and start seeing people," she would say, and Lesley knew
that she was right.

The first week that she had been back to Clifton she had
stayed in her room, sleeping and crying, convinced that she
would die. But for the last five weeks she had been busy
every day, doing errands, visiting old friends and looking
for a job.

A friendly hand on her shoulder pulled her out of her
daydreams, and she lifted her head to look up at the man
standing next to her. "Hello, Todd," she said, smiling at
the even, almost pretty features of the big blond man.

"Hello there, Lesley Belmont. You're looking like a
picture in an advertisement for soft drinks."

She smiled in acknowledgment of the compliment.
Wearing tight khaki shorts and a copper colored tank top
that hugged every curve of her body, Lesley knew that she
looked good. The moist heat of the June day had curled
her hair around her face and her recent afternoons in the
sun helping her father weed his garden had tanned her skin
to a rich golden brown. Smiling lazily at the big man she
leaned casually against the counter with her hands perched
on her hips.

"You look like summer is going to get the best of you in
that outfit," she replied. Reaching forward, she straightened the tie that was a perfect match for the well-tailored
three-piece suit he was wearing.

"I have a conference in Chapel Hill this afternoon and
I have to wear this monkey suit. You can bet my car air
conditioner will be on full blast all the way." His eyes

swept over Lesley appreciatively. "I'm planning to be back late this afternoon. Would you like to go out to dinner with me? There's a new barbecue place that just opened up a few miles down the highway and I'd like to try it with you."

She grinned at him and chuckled softly.

He smiled back, a little warily. "Was that funny?"

Lesley shook her head slightly, chuckling still. "No, but I was just thinking that I would have died of sheer pleasure in high school if you had asked me out."

"If I had asked you out in high school, honey, you'd have bitten my head off." Todd arched his brow. "You were just about the scariest girl I ever knew."

"Scary?" She almost choked on the adjective. "Scary?"

"That's right, honey. You were so smart, so perfect, that nobody wanted to take a chance on being shown up by you. It was a shame too, because we all noticed..."

Lesley narrowed her eyes slightly. "Noticed what?"

"Well, that is to say, we all couldn't help but notice how nicely you, uh...developed."

She looked at him with a startled grin. "You're kidding."

"Nope. I'm not. How about that dinner?"

Nodding her head, she didn't notice that he took her hand and raised it to his lips. "What time?"

"About eight. And Lesley, we can talk about that job teaching English. I think you have a really good chance at it."

"Todd," she said slowly as he turned around to walk out the door, "my performance tonight doesn't count for or against me, does it?"

He pulled himself up and glared at her, only to wink lecherously when he saw she wasn't impressed. "Naw, it doesn't count. I may be a dirty old principal, but I draw the line at that. You'll have a chance to see how professional I can be."

Lesley continued to lean against the counter watching him walk down the sunny sidewalk. Todd Wilson had been Mr. Big at Clifton High School. Captain of this, president of that, Most Likely to.... Now he was the principal of the very same school and doing an excellent job from what she had been told. Recently divorced from a woman who had been president of the pep club in Lesley's senior year, he was considered the hottest catch in town. The irony of the situation filled her with delight. For a moment she almost forgot the pain curled up like a sleeping tiger inside her.

Wishing that she could avoid playing these games, Lesley mentally compared Todd with Travis Hagen. "Don't," she whispered, but the comparison flooded insistently through her mind. Travis, whose features were no less perfect but so much more masculine. Travis, whose body next to hers could create small hurricanes inside her. Travis, who could turn her to Jell-O with one casual, sexy look. And Travis, she told herself firmly, who had thought she was a terrific target for humiliation.

Purchasing the items she needed, Lesley began to walk home along the tree-shaded main street. Once she was away from the shopping district, the sidewalks turned into paths and she smiled and waved at people working in their front yards and at children playing under the shade of magnolias or pines.

For an indecisive moment, she stood on the corner of a street running downhill to a small creek. Jennifer and David had a house facing the little creek, and Lesley considered dropping in to see them. Thinking better of it she continued on to her parents' home. The old, white, two-story frame house sat on the crest of a slight hill and Lesley looked up and waved at her mother who was watching her.

Mary Jane Belmont was sitting on the front porch in a tall wooden rocking chair, and she patted the seat of the chair next to her as an invitation to Lesley. Pouring her a glass of iced tea from a tray on a small table next to them, Mrs. Belmont sighed and began to fan herself.

"It's going to be a scorcher, Lesley. Your dad is in our room taking a nap with the air conditioner on. I worry about him in this heat." Her good-natured, plump face didn't look worried, and Lesley knew that the fretting was part of her personality.

"Dad's looking good, mom. I worried about him a lot when I was in...Virginia." She paused with a slight catch in her voice. "But now that I see how well he's doing, I feel a lot better."

They sat in silence, watching the occasional person passing by the porch. The rich perfume of honeysuckle dominated the heated air and Lesley was flooded with memories of her childhood. She put her head back and sighed contentedly.

"You're doing better, aren't you, sweetie?" There was no idle curiosity in Mrs. Belmont's tone. Real concern hung in the air as poignant as the honeysuckle, and Lesley allowed it to settle over her. The feeling was familiar and warming. She was glad she had decided to come home.

"Yes, I think I am. I even heard myself singing today. I haven't done that in weeks." She turned slightly to meet her mother's eyes. "I still hurt terribly, and I wonder if it will ever go away, but I don't feel like I'm dying anymore. Does that make sense?"

Mrs. Belmont took a deep breath, a curiously radiant expression shining in her faded-blue eyes, and she reached to touch Lesley's cheek. "I think the last time you shared your feelings with me was when you were six years old and your best friend didn't invite you to her birthday party. I can't tell you how nice it is to have you here right now."

Lesley felt a sharp ache for the little woman sitting next to her. "Mother, I'm sorry...I didn't mean to be..."

"Hush, Lesley. You have no reason to apologize for anything. You've been a wonderful daughter. It's just that I always wanted to get close and was never sure how to do it." She wiped her eyes surreptitiously on the sleeve of her dress. "You've always been so self-sufficient I was never sure you needed anyone. Since you've been home this time, I've seen that isn't true."

Lesley shut her eyes, momentarily overwhelmed with pain and longing. "No, that certainly isn't true." She opened her eyes and looked at her mother. "I'm lucky to have a family to get me through this."

"Are you ready to tell me what happened?" Mrs. Belmont's voice was even, but Lesley sensed the deep longing to provide solace. Briefly she told her mother the story, leaving out no details.

"And that's why you won't take Travis Hagen's phone calls."

"That's right," Lesley answered tersely. "I never want to talk to him again."

"He's been remarkably persistent for a young man who only has a guilty conscience he wants to clear up, sweetie. Do you think maybe he's got something else to tell you? Perhaps your information isn't correct."

Lesley flinched as she thought of the phone calls that she had refused to answer since her return to North Carolina. "He's stopped now. Whatever was motivating him doesn't seem to be motivating him now."

She glanced at her mother and saw a guilty look steal across the otherwise wholesome features. "Mother, has Travis Hagen been bothering you?"

"No, he's not bothering me." Mrs. Belmont got up as if to head back into the house. "I'll just check on your father, I think."

Lesley reached out and caught her mother's wrist as Mrs. Belmont reached for the iced-tea glasses. "Mother, sit." Mrs. Belmont sat, looking uncomfortable. "What are you up to, mother?" Lesley asked, her voice as cold as the tea had been.

"Just when I thought we were about to break through all those barriers." Mrs. Belmont sighed.

"Mother!"

With the look that Napoleon must have worn at Waterloo, Mrs. Belmont gave up her pretenses. "After about the fourteenth phone call, Travis said he was coming down here to see you whether you wanted to see him or not."

"Damn Gerald!"

"Gerald?" Mrs. Belmont was bewildered.

"That's the only place he could have gotten my whereabouts from. Gerald's secretary, Sylvia...never mind, go on."

"Travis said..."

"Travis! You're calling him Travis? What is going on here?"

"Travis said," Mrs. Belmont continued patiently, "that he was going to come down and get you and wring your pretty little neck. I think those were his exact words."

Lesley sputtered. "That arrogant, cruel, demeaning..."

"I told him that you wanted to be left alone. That you were very hurt and needed some time to think. I convinced him to stop calling for a while and give you room to breathe."

Lesley watched her mother with a calculating look. "Why do I think you're not quite done talking yet?"

Mrs. Belmont looked embarrassed. "Well, there's only a little more."

"Give."

"I've been calling him weekly to let him know how you're doing." She cringed momentarily at the look on Lesley's face. "He's been very worried, sweetie. He seems like such a nice man."

"Nice?" Lesley stood up and stomped over to the porch railing. "Nice? That's like calling a boa constrictor a cute little snake! It's like calling King Kong a sweet little monkey! It's like calling... Oh mother, how could you?"

"Someday, you'll thank me, dear," Mrs. Belmont said tamely as she got up to take the glasses in the house. She turned at the doorway. "You know, I haven't seen you lose your temper in twenty years. It's very becoming."

Lesley stared at the swinging screen door. Revelations were being slung at her today that made her head spin. Evidently things were not as they had always seemed. The fact that her mother had viewed her as a self-sufficient, controlled person who was difficult to approach was hard to fathom. The way the boys at school had viewed her as too smart to get close to, even if they were interested in the way she had "uh...developed" was astounding. The fact that Travis Hagen, damn his hide, was still in her life whether she wanted him there or not was outrageous.

Lesley put her fingers to her temples, slowly massaging away the tension there. Life was difficult enough without finding out that all the premises she had built on were incorrect.

"Hey, sis, how's it going?" She looked up to see her sister climbing the steps with her youngest son, Troy. And here was a case in point, she thought as she watched Jennifer.

Lesley gave Jennifer a quick hug, and ruffled five-year-old Troy's blond hair casually. "Hello, you two."

Troy skipped off to find his grandparents and Jennifer plopped down in the seat on the porch and began to fan herself briskly. Lesley got a sudden vision of what Jennifer would look like in twenty years. Mary Jane Belmont had sat in that seat only moments before doing the same thing, with the same look on her face. Jennifer, the popular cheerleader, the beauty queen, the cute and perky high school success story, had turned into an almost plump, frowsy, younger version of her mother. The realization did not make Lesley love her any less, but once again she realized that she had been operating on information that was not correct.

"What do you think, Lesley?" Jennifer's lilting voice was serious as she watched Lesley color faintly.

"I was staring, wasn't I?" She grinned wryly at Jennifer's nod. "I'll be honest. I was just thinking that I've spent my whole life operating on one set of assumptions and I'm finding out that a lot of them weren't true."

"Are you finally noticing that I'm just a normal person and not some sort of mythical goddess?"

Lesley nodded. "I've spent most of my life thinking that if I were you, everything would be all right." She hastened to add, "Not that I was jealous exactly; I just couldn't figure out why there couldn't be two of you. And then along came Maribeth and I found out that there could be, but one of them wasn't going to be me."

Jennifer laughed softly. "I think I know what you mean. You wanted to be little and cute and blond. I know because I wanted to be tall and have curly hair and be valedictorian of the class."

"You're kidding."

Jennifer put her hand in back of her head, five wiggling fingers protruding as she recited:

As a Cherokee Indian maid
No club promises will be betrayed
If I tell a lie than I
Will at sunrise surely die.

Lesley reminisced with a gurgling laugh. "We were six, eight and ten. I was secretary, you were president, and Maribeth was a pain in the neck. I'd almost forgotten."

"We had a good time as children here, didn't we? But really, Lesley, I'm not sure that anyone ever is satisfied with who they are when they're growing up." She reached over and patted Lesley on the hand. "I've always wanted to tell you that."

"Are you happy with your life now?" Lesley asked wistfully, linking her long fingers with Jennifer's shorter ones.

"I'm as happy as any person has a right to be. I know I'm not glamorous or well educated or exciting. But David is a great husband and the children give me such pleasure. Sometimes I envy you your freedom and your involvement in your job. That's natural, I guess. But I'm satisfied. I don't look backward much." She gave Lesley's hand a squeeze. "And you? Happiness is eluding you right now, isn't it?"

Lesley nodded, a lump forming in her throat. "Yes, but I think I may be beginning to understand why. The difference between us was never that you were short and I was tall. Or that you were cheerleader material while I was a born valedictorian. The difference was that you weren't afraid to go after what you wanted. I was. And the one time I did go for it, I used very poor judgment."

"You're talking about a man, aren't you?"

Lesley nodded in silence.

"And now?"

Lesley sighed, returning Jennifer's squeeze as she withdrew her hand. "I think that I've changed, Jennifer. I'm going to try and never be frightened to be what I want to be, do what I want to do."

"Good for you," Jennifer slapped her sister lightly on the knee. "Does that mean you're going to go back to Virginia and straighten out whatever is wrong there?"

Lesley grimaced. "Not a chance."

Shaking her head, Jennifer got up to go in the house. "You've got a ways to go then. But you're coming along. You're definitely coming along."

Getting dressed that night for her dinner with Todd, Lesley discovered that she could not stop thinking about Travis and what it would be like if she were going out with him. She knew that she would suffer for her fantasies that night when she climbed into bed. She had discovered after her first week at home that if she spent the day keeping busy, interacting with her family, doing any form of hard physical labor, she could usually get through the night without the bad dreams that centered on her betrayal by the man she had come to love.

Today Travis had been in her thoughts too much. The comparisons with Todd, her confessions to her mother and the news that Travis was keeping in touch with her via phone calls to Mrs. Belmont, had all served to knock down the fragile walls that Lesley had built to protect herself. Memories had come rushing in that she could not stifle.

One-dimensional memories might be easier to handle, but her memories of Travis were all three-dimensional. There were no wisps of conversations, clouded visions or dreamlike reminiscences. In her mind and in her heart, Travis lived and breathed in full living color complete with sound, smell, touch, and taste. Remembered clearly were full discussions, whispered words of passion and the delicious sensations of his body against hers.

"I'm asking for a nightmare tonight," she whispered as she forced herself to continue dressing. At Jennifer's urging, Lesley had shopped for some new summer clothing and now she chose one of her new dresses to wear to dinner. The creamy gold gauze was embroidered with tiny green and brown butterflies around the halter neckline, and the color emphasized her new tan. The back of the sundress plunged to a point several vertebrae lower than she was comfortable with, but Jennifer had insisted and Lesley had to admit that it was very cool that way.

She brushed her hair until it shone and curled smoothly around her shoulders, then lightly glossed her lips and used a touch of blusher to highlight her cheekbones. She had grown accustomed to her new image in the full-length mirror, but she still smiled when she saw how nice she looked in the gold dress. For a short time after arriving home, she had tried to return to her dowdy self, sure that she could avoid unnecessary pain that way. But that attempt had lasted only a few days. She'd awakened one morning and realized that she was a caricature of her true self. She decided then and there that she didn't want to go through life looking like Lily in "The Family Jones" and the local charity thrift shop had received a bonanza of navy blue skirts and plain white blouses that day.

The doorbell rang, and Lesley grabbed a soft olive-green shawl that Jennifer had bought for her to wear with the dress. Todd was chatting comfortably with her parents when she walked down to meet him. She smiled at his appreciative whistle and gave her parents a hug. Settled satisfactorily on the seat of the little Datsun that Todd drove, she could feel herself relax by inches. They listened to old Beatles songs on the car stereo and talked casually about their lives since high school.

When they reached the restaurant, Todd took Lesley's arm and helped her out of the car. By that time, she felt so comfortable with him that she didn't even notice when he failed to let go of it. They ordered platters of spareribs and sat drinking sugar-saturated iced tea from gigantic mason jars as they picked at the salads they had mixed for themselves from the elaborate salad bar.

"This was just what I needed, Todd," Lesley said as she looked around the rustic little room.

"Didn't they feed you barbecue up north?"

She smiled at his characterization of Virginia. "I meant the company, just being with a friend. This is fun."

Todd looked at her appraisingly. "Then we'll have to do it often. I think it's fun too."

Their ribs arrived, and between trying to eat without splattering themselves with sauce and trying to find out about each other, the evening flew by. And if there was a treacherous voice inside Lesley that consistently tried to remind her of Travis, she fought it down as best she could.

Todd kissed her good-night on the front porch after a long drive through the country, the night air blowing through the open windows and the sunroof in his car. The kiss was sweet and old-fashioned, nothing like she would have expected from the wolf of Clifton High, but now that wolf was the principal and she was about to become the newly hired English teacher. As she watched him walk toward his car, Lesley shrugged her shoulders at the surprises life constantly offered.

The phone was ringing when she walked through the door and without thinking she picked it up, hoping that it hadn't disturbed her parents.

"Lesley?" She stiffened at the familiar voice.

"What do you want, Gerald?" Lesley moved her finger to the little button that could cut him off in one second if he became abusive. "It's late and I have no desire whatsoever to have a conversation with you about anything."

"I'm sure you don't, and I don't blame you." Gerald's tone was even and calm. "Please let me talk to you for a minute, though. I really need to."

Suspicion blazed through Lesley like wildfire in a pine forest as she found the little stool that her mother kept in the corner by the phone and perched cautiously on it. "What is this about, Gerald?"

There was an audible sigh on the other end of the line. Lesley waited, her finger creeping back to the phone. "I'm not sure where to begin, but maybe I ought to start with the safest part and tell you that your job is still open. I never submitted your letter of resignation to the dean. As far as they know, you're on an extended leave of absence."

"That's unrealistic, Gerald," she said formally. "I'm certainly not planning to come back. Shall I send a letter to the dean myself?"

"If you decide you must. But I'm going to leave the opening for a few more days. I want you to think about coming back. We need you here." There was a slight pause as he seemed to grapple with what to say next.

She spared him the agony. "No."

"Lesley, I've made some...changes. After you left things began to pile up. I realized that you were right about me. I was living in an alcoholic haze. I've had a lot of help and I'm not out of the woods yet, but I believe that I can lick this problem." There was a note of pride in his voice. "I haven't touched a drink in a month. I know that's not a long time, but I don't plan to drink ever again."

Lesley weighed his words. "Why are you telling me this, Gerald? Do you think that will change my feelings about you?"

"Not in the way you mean." He sounded so sincere and Lesley was surprised to find that she believed him. "I'd like to know that you will gain back some respect from me, but that's all I'd ever expect. Actually, I've become involved with someone since you left. She's helped me through the most difficult times."

Lesley smiled at the embarrassment in his voice. "But Gerald, that's great. Anybody I know?"

He hesitated. "Well, yes. It's Sylvia."

"Sylvia," she squealed into the phone. "Sylvia?"

"Some surprise, huh?"

"Some surprise. Someday I want to hear this story from beginning to end."

"Come back and we'll sit you down and tell you all the romantic details. Really, Lesley. Everyone misses you here. And I happen to know that a certain comic strip artist is at the head of the list."

The warmth Lesley had been feeling after hearing Gerald's news faded immediately. "Leave Travis Hagen out of this."

"I'd be glad to but your Mr. Hagen won't let me. He comes by frequently to see if we've got any news about you. In fact, he and Sylvia are hitting it off so well, I'm getting jealous."

"She's welcome to both of you," Lesley said shortly.

"Only to me, my dear. Travis Hagen has ideas of his own on that score."

They talked for another minute, and Lesley hung up feeling amazed once again. Gerald certainly sounded like a changed man. Love seemed to do wonderful things for people. She had a sharp twinge realizing that the research she loved so much and the friends she had made in Virginia, and even Gerald, were completely out of her life now. There was definitely a temptation to go back to her old job. But the reality of a certain man loomed over her, and she knew that she would never be able to go back again.

"Damn you, Travis Hagen!"

Wrenching off her sandals she stalked silently up the stairs, closing the door of her room firmly behind her. She sat on the bed looking around at the ultrafeminine decorations that Jennifer and Maribeth had loved so. Pink ruffled curtains hung at the window. Lilac and pink flowered bedspreads covered the three single beds sitting neatly in a row. Vivian might not approve, but it was home.

Undressing slowly, she put on a white terry cloth robe and went into the bathroom to run a hot bath. She waited until the tub was ready before climbing in and stayed until the water was so cold she was uncomfortable. Toweling herself dry she took an inordinately long time massaging face cream into her glowing skin and then wiping it off again. Next she brushed her teeth, carefully and thoroughly, flossing them took longer than usual because she decided to do each tooth twice. Finally she sighed and left the bathroom, immaculately clean but still terrified of the long night ahead.

Back in her room she prowled through the bookcases for a book to keep her company. The titles were from her childhood and adolescence. She was in no mood for *Black Beauty* or *Little Women*. The Nancy Drew series looked even less appealing and with a certain anxiety Lesley climbed into bed convinced that sleep was going to have to be her next plan.

Surprisingly she fell asleep quickly. She tossed and turned fretfully through the night, but it wasn't until early morning that the nightmare began. It started on the beach in the sunshine with Travis. They had spread a soft blanket on the sparkling sand and they were lying side by side, not touching but looking longingly at each other. The dream was vivid, and Lesley could hear the pounding of the turf and the squawking of the sea gulls.

Travis turned to her and propped his head on his hand. As he bent to kiss her they heard a noise. Coming down the beach toward them were T.J., Vivian, Gerald, Sylvia and a smiling blond man. Travis leapt up and ran toward them, but Lesley found that she couldn't move. She cried out for help, but everyone walked past her, unseeing, uncaring. Watching helplessly she saw Vivian and the blond man continue hand in hand down the beach. Gerald and Travis began to play catch with a colorful beach ball. Sylvia stood nearby holding T.J.'s hand and watching them as they played.

Lesley tried to sit up, to call out, but no one paid her any attention. In frustration she moaned and Travis and Gerald came over to the blanket to bury her in the sand, at first playfully, and then with real malice. She tried to scream, but the sand filled her mouth and she was mute.

She awoke to find herself sitting up, trying to push the covers off the bed as great gulping sobs shook her body. Sitting there wrapped in the sheets that she had tried so hard to discard, she faced the fact that she had not even begun to touch the misery she felt at Travis's betrayal. Life had to go on, she had to adjust, but there was a very real possibility that she might never be able to think about Travis again without bringing this pain upon herself.

There was no point in trying to fall back to sleep. She went to sit on the flowered window seat under the front window of her room. The sun was just beginning to come up, and the morning darkness was slowly being highlighted by fingers of twirling sunlight. There had been other mornings in her life when she had sat here, knees drawn up to cradle her head, staring out at the world which held such mysteries.

The dream haunted her although the terror she'd felt began to dissipate. Painfully she reworked it. The beginning had been so promising, just like her relationship with Travis. She recognized the setting from the picture that Travis had painted and hung in his bedroom. There had been a moment in the dream when Vivian and the blond man had turned and walked away and it was exactly like the scene in Travis's picture. She knew that the man in the picture was Joshua, Vivian's lost love. Why the picture had figured in Lesley's dream she wasn't sure, except that it portrayed the same loneliness she had felt since coming back to North Carolina.

The rest of the dream was only too clear. All that promise had turned to ashes. Travis had betrayed her, at first as a joke, finally as a terrible vindictive prank. The dream mirrored her feelings. She felt helpless, silent, unable to communicate to anyone the depth of her betrayal.

Lesley curled up on the seat and covered herself with the lilac afghan which lay folded and waiting for just such a moment. Facing the meaning of the dream had not been easy, but she knew that it was the only way to banish it. Humiliated that she could still care so much, she was also proud of her ability to explore her feelings and try to deal with them. There was a hollow space inside her but she felt a blessed numbness beginning to creep over her. In a few minutes she was asleep again.

The dream returned. She was on the beach with Travis and he was bending over to kiss her. As they heard the noises of people on the beach approaching them, Travis leaned down and whispered in her ear. "Trust me. I would never hurt you. Trust me."

"I know," she answered.

The dream ended. Lesley, fated not to remember the dream when she awoke, slept on.

## Chapter Ten

The envelope was propped next to Lesley's glass of orange juice when she went downstairs to breakfast the next morning. It was a big fat one, the type that carried more than a few pages of friendly chitchat, and it didn't take much detective work to figure out who it was from. Circling the oversized cream-colored stationery was a brilliant rainbow. "The Rainbow Connection" and Vivian's address were printed in gay violet script in the corner.

Piled on top of the fatigue of a restless night, the envelope was too much. Lesley pitched it across the room where it landed on the kitchen counter, narrowly missing the platter of bacon and eggs. Her mouth dropped open in astonishment, and she looked at her mother in dismay.

"Mmm...that temper is becoming, dear, but I think if it interferes with your father's breakfast it could be a problem." Mrs. Belmont tactfully left the room as Lesley sat down at the table and put her head in her hands. There really was no excuse for that kind of behavior and she would apologize as soon as she got herself under control. Now if I could only manage to do that in the next decade, she thought sadly.

Her parents came in a few moments later to join her for breakfast and her mother patted her hand in response to Lesley's pleading smile. Mr. Belmont was cheerfully looking forward to a day of fishing in his favorite stream, and on a whim, Mrs. Belmont decided to join him. Lesley politely refused their offer to take her along, and shooed them both out of the kitchen as she began to clean up after their meal.

She picked up her plate and scraped the food into the garbage can. It was virtually untouched, and she watched the quivering eggs slide off the plate and onto a heap of coffee grounds. There was something touching about those eggs. Some little chicken somewhere had laid them, and she, Lesley Belmont, hadn't even had the decency to eat them. Laying eggs couldn't be easy, she thought empathetically, and she hadn't even given them a reason for existence. A tear trickled down her nose.

"My God," she said out loud. "I'm crying over the garbage." The tears continued and she grabbed a handful of napkins to mop up the flood. "I'm losing my mind." Since returning to North Carolina she had found herself crying over the simplest things. Once an old sixties song, "The Leader of the Pack," had come on the radio and when the young heroine lost her lover, Lesley had cried through the next five selections. Another time she found herself weeping when a blue jay flew by dangling an earth worm from his beak.

The tears began to give way to snorts and finally grunts of laughter. In a moment she was alternately crying and laughing, not quite out of control, but fast approaching that condition. With an effort of will she gulped several mouthfuls of air, and slowed the torrent down to a mere trickle.

She finished clearing the table, her knees weak from her emotional display, but now she felt better. She was glad to see that she could still laugh at herself. She began putting away dishes and food, washing things as she went. Pinching Vivian's letter with her thumb and index finger, she moved it back to the table. The envelope was heavy, and it apparently contained enclosures, because it was also bulky. Ignoring the twinge of curiosity that she was beginning to feel, Lesley finished the cleanup and went upstairs to change into shorts and a halter top. Today she would sunbathe, relax and try to forget the misery she was feeling.

Lying outside in the relentless morning sun, she came to the conclusion that there must be a better way to spend the day. Already bathed in sweat, she felt no desire to roast any longer. Sighing, she bundled up the spread and suntan lotion and went back indoors. She took a long cool shower, toweled herself off thoroughly, changed into a fresh lime-green playsuit, and checked the clock. "Ten-thirty?" Sitting on the window seat and gazing out the window she wondered if the rest of her life was going to be a series of maneuvers designed to waste time.

Since leaving home at age eighteen, Lesley had watched almost no television. With a sigh of resignation she went downstairs to the living room and turned on the big color console that was her mother's pride and joy. She grimaced at the game show announcer and turned the channel. The silver-haired talk show host was discussing menopause and she grimaced again. A commercial for cat food on the last channel was so trite that she flicked it off in disgust.

Heading into the kitchen for a tall glass of iced tea, Lesley caught sight of Vivian's letter on the table. If she continued to avoid reading it, she could waste the entire day pretending that she didn't care. She picked it up and her trembling fingers convinced her that it was definitely time to quit stalling. She was not casual; she was not angry; she was just plain scared. And the time to face that fear was now.

She retreated with the letter in hand to the living room where she settled into her father's big plaid armchair. Balancing the letter on her fingertips, she imagined all the possibilities contained within it. Maybe the envelope was heavy because Vivian had sent her some new color swatches. Impossible. Maybe the envelope held clippings about T.J.'s prowess on the baseball field. Unlikely. Maybe Vivian was writing to gloat. Lesley realized that this was the biggest terror of all. She did not want to believe that Vivian had been part of all of this too. Travis had betrayed her trust, and Lesley wasn't sure she could handle Vivian's betrayal too.

And yet it seemed likely to her, in her depression, that Vivian might be glad to have her out of the way. Perhaps she was interested in making a fresh start with Travis. The three of them—T.J., Travis and Vivian—could be a family again. The pain of that possibility stabbed her brutally. It was time to open the letter.

She blanched when she saw the enclosures. A neatly clipped series of comic strips lay in her lap. As Lesley had predicted before coming, none of the papers that she had access to in Clifton carried "The Family Jones," and she had been spared the daily agony of watching the story unfold. Now Vivian had sent the strips to rub her nose in her misery. Enclosed with them was a letter, written carefully in a delicate script that matched so well the delicate beauty of its owner. Lesley steeled herself to read the letter. It was short and to the point.

Dear Lesley,

My first thought is that you will see this letter as an interference in your life. I hope you will forgive me for it really is just that. I found out several weeks ago that you had left Virginia and although Travis refuses to talk about your reason, I think I can guess what might have caused your abrupt departure.

I am enclosing copies of "The Family Jones" for you to read in the hope that you will look at them carefully for the message that they contain.

All I can hope is that you will view this act in the spirit that it is meant. I value your friendship.

Yours,
Vivian Alexander

There were no more tears, Lesley thought, although this was the perfect opportunity to cry some. She had wasted her tears on a chicken and an egg. She was empty except for the trembling inside her when she looked at the comic strips piled carelessly on her lap. They seemed to burn a hole in the tender skin of her thigh, and she thought seriously about heaving them across the room. But she had wasted her anger on an envelope that morning, and there was no more left. It was time to face the inevitable.

Beginning with the first strip, she suffered through the same ten strips that she had read in Virginia before she had decided to take Travis's car and leave for good. She relived the pain of those moments as once again she saw the awkward character of Lily, fumbling around, making mistakes, trying to avoid any contact with the suave country bachelor, Bubba Jones.

She reluctantly went on to the next strip, and the next. There was a subtle change occurring in both characters, and even in her misery she was able to see it. She read on.

Lily was being transformed from an awkward, shy spinster into a glowing, attractive woman. Bubba was being transformed from a womanizing, slick country dude to a caring, concerned admirer of her beauty. But the change was not so much physical, although the glasses and the self-conscious bun were gone. The change was almost spiritual: the merging of two parts of a whole, the giving of trust, the awakening of love.

Lesley read the last strip with tears in her eyes, tears that she had thought were all used up. In the strip, Bubba held Lily and kissed her for the first time, and in the background, Grandpa Silas Jones looked on with an expression as understanding and as radiant as the sun bursting through cloudy skies after a rainstorm. There would be more episodes, perhaps another conflict or two, but it was obvious that love had bloomed in "The Family Jones," and that Lily was there to stay.

Paralyzed by her discovery, Lesley sat quietly in the big armchair. She had been wrong, terribly wrong. She tried to summon her anger back. How dare Travis use her as a caricature. To strengthen her point, she went back over the first part of the episode. There was the bun, the glasses, the too-long skirts, and the too-tailored blouses. But to her dismay, she realized suddenly that there was where the unattractiveness lay.

Lily was not ugly. She was shy; the choice of clothes seemed to be trying to cover up her shyness. Any awkwardness that was displayed by her was also displayed by Bubba, who didn't seem to know how to act around this unassuming, modest woman. In certain frames of the strip, Travis had highlighted Lily's face, giving her the appearance of a quiet madonna. And later, when her hair was loose around her shoulders and the glasses were gone, her beauty, both inner and outer, was a real focal point of the strip.

How could she summon up anger, when it was suddenly apparent that there was nothing to be angry about? No anger, no humiliation, no betrayal. Travis's love for her shone through every frame of the little comic strip. Lesley had been a fool. Her lack of self-esteem had completely colored her initial reading of the series. There was no ridicule there. And yet she had jumped to the conclusion again that she was being made fun of.

The realization of the truth was like a light bulb over the head of a character in a comic strip of the past. She had brought her misery on herself. Entirely on herself. No one had helped her; no one had caused her pain. Singlehandedly she had destroyed the most important thing in her life: the love that she shared with Travis Hagen. And as surely as she understood now that she had been entirely at fault, she also understood the depth of Travis's feelings for her. He loved her, as Vivian had loved Joshua, as Bubba loved Lily. Or perhaps, she thought miserably, Travis had loved her once. After what she had done, it was doubtful if he felt anything for her except contempt.

"What have I done?" she moaned out loud.

When she stood up to pace the length of the room fretfully, the comic strips tumbled off her lap to float gently to the floor. She picked them up tenderly and held them to her cheek. They were visible signs of the feelings that Travis had once had for her. They wouldn't be much use on a cold winter night, but perhaps some afternoon when she was an old lady, she'd pull them out of a secret box and remember her lost love.

She pictured the scene. Jennifer's great-grandchildren would be up in the attic of Lesley's little white house in Clifton, which by then would probably be a bustling metropolis. They would be dressed in old clothes, dresses too long, hats too big. Tiring of the game of dress-up in the quaint old house, they would begin looking through the bundles of ancient letters tied with faded ribbons. "What are these, Great-aunt Lesley?" they would ask, holding up the packet of yellowed comic strips. "Ah...those are from my youth," she would murmur in a cracking old lady's voice. "Those were done by my lost love."

"Lost love, my eyeball!" she shrieked. "I've really lost my mind." The time had come for her to take action. Only so much could be accomplished by well-meaning friends and relatives. It was her life, her decision. And the time to act was now.

With a leap that stopped slightly short of being a world record, she was out of the living room and running up the stairs. She stopped briefly in the hallway to make a quick phone call and then continued on to her bedroom. Pulling her suitcases out of the closet, she began to throw her clothes into them, stopping only to select a fiery orange sundress with a low neckline and an even lower back. "Thank you, Jennifer," she breathed gratefully, remembering Jennifer's insistence when Lesley had wavered about buying the dress.

Thanks to her donation to the thrift store, she found that she had little packing to do. She finished in record time, dressing quickly in the seductively revealing dress, and applying makeup with a more lavish than usual hand. Catching her hair over one ear with an ivory comb, she decided the effect was just right.

Scrawling a quick goodbye to her parents, she placed the little note over the kitchen sink where her mother was sure to see it immediately. She threw the suitcases in the car and backed out of the driveway.

The man sitting next to Lesley on the airplane spent the entire flight, short though it was, trying to charm her into agreeing to go out with him when they arrived in Roanoke. Her flat refusals seemed to interest him as much as the voluptuous cleavage that the halter dress hinted at. Lesley enjoyed the encounter thoroughly. Under any other circumstances his massive frame and curly hair would have been immensely appealing. Today, however, she could only think about penetrating blue eyes, a lean muscular body and the shiny brown hair that consistently skimmed the forehead of the man she loved.

She had almost missed the plane, running through the terminal at the last minute to find the correct gate to board the flight, which was the only one to Roanoke that day. The excitement of the chase, the encounter with her seatmate, and her natural anxiety at having to confront Travis later in the day had her in a fever pitch of emotion. Her cheeks were flushed, her eyes were sparkling, and she felt that every nerve ending was on fire. When the flight attendant announced their imminent landing, she rattled in anticipation.

Firmly refusing the help of her seatmate, she stood up and walked shakily down the aisle. She would rent a car, she decided, and drive to Travis's house. With any luck at all she would find him there and she could apologize to him for her stupidity. Beyond that, she dared not hope for anything else.

Lesley walked down the long metal steps into the bright, hot sunshine of a Blue Ridge summer day. Walking across the field she drank in the sight of the surrounding mountains. This was her heart's home. Here her spirit felt at rest; her need for beauty was assuaged. Stopping momentarily and gazing out across the field, she knew that she would not leave again. She would call Gerald tomorrow and tell him that she wanted her job back. And she would call Todd and tell him that she was withdrawing her name as a candidate for the teaching job at Clifton High. No matter what happened with Travis today, she would not run away again. She was done with that part of her life.

She quickly covered the distance across the field. Inside the modest building she watched the other passengers being greeted by loved ones. Kisses were being exchanged freely, relatives were crying, children were pushing and shoving. Lesley wished suddenly that she was not standing there alone.

A prickling sensation at the back of her neck alerted her to the fact that someone was staring at her. Turning slightly to reassure her overheated imagination that she was mistaken, she saw the tall figure of a man lounging against the wall of the terminal, apart from the crowd. In faded blue jeans and a sapphire-blue cotton shirt unbuttoned at the top to reveal a shiny medallion, the man looked like a sun god, a prototype for Apollo. Pushing away from the wall, he ran his fingers through his fine brown hair and succeeded in brushing it off his forehead for just a moment.

Lesley sucked her breath in as Travis approached her. They stood and stared at each other, oblivious to the crowd around them. The words of apology that she had mentally rehearsed during the trip deserted her. She could only stare unblinkingly into the endless depths of his eyes.

There was no smile on Travis's face. He stood there patiently watching her, receiving but not returning the longing in her eyes. She had never seen Travis when his expression was impossible to read, but today his normally mobile features were blank, neither condemning nor welcoming. The heavy-lidded eyes were shuttered, closed off to her. The heat radiating from his body wove an invisible web around her. She wanted to reach out and touch him to break through the barrier between them, but she knew instinctively that her touch would not be welcomed.

"How did you know I was coming, Travis?" Her voice was barely audible in the noisy room.

"Your mother called me. Evidently you left North Carolina as suddenly as you left Virginia. She was worried about you." His voice, like his expression, gave nothing away.

"I planned to call her as soon as I landed. There was no time to talk to anyone if I was going to catch this flight."

Travis reached around and took her by the elbow to guide her across the room to the pay telephones there. "I'll wait," he said tersely. "Mary Jane was quite worried. You have a very bad habit of scaring people, Lesley."

He dropped her elbow as she reached inside her purse for change to make the phone call. The skin, where he had lightly held her arm, felt tingly from his touch. With a sinking heart she prophesied silently that those few inches of skin might be the last ones on her body ever touched by Travis Hagen. She dialed the correct codes and number, stopping when her mother answered the phone to deposit the enormous amount of change that was required. Travis stood by passively.

When she hung up after reassuring her mother, Lesley turned back to where Travis had been standing. He was no longer there, and for one wild moment she was sure that he had only come to do his duty and ease her mother's concern for her before he had gone back home. She looked around frantically to see him coming from the direction of the coffee shop, carrying covered cups and a small paper bag.

"Mary Jane said you probably hadn't eaten all day. This is for you."

"Bologna?" she said, trying for a light touch.

He humphed at her and she opened up the bag to find a mangled club sandwich.

He looked at it and for one split second, a grin broke through. "I shouldn't have carried it under my arm, right?"

"It looks just great, Travis, thank you." She stood there in the large room, holding the sandwich and coffee that he had presented her with, her gaze never leaving his face.

"Well, you can't eat it here." He motioned to the orange and blue chairs in the corner. Settling down in the pseudocomfort to eat, Lesley found herself mentally rehearsing her apologies as she chewed the compressed ham and turkey sandwich.

"Well, at least it will take me less time to eat it, now that you've flattened it for me," she chuckled softly.

"Are we going to spend the afternoon talking about that stupid sandwich?" Travis asked with a spurt of exasperation.

"Travis," she said, setting the coffee on the floor beside her, "I'm so very sorry." She looked up to find him watching her, his blank expression still intact. "I suspected you of some pretty awful things. I was wrong."

"Is that all?" His look would qualify as a sneer on a less appealing face, she thought with a sinking heart.

"What else can I say? I feel terrible about what happened." Lesley had a sudden desire to find the ladies' room and dump the sandwich and herself into the waste paper basket.

"You can give me an explanation, that's what! I think I have an inkling of what went wrong, but I want to hear every blasted detail of it right from your pretty mouth."

He was right. At the very least she owed him that much, and yet the thought of rehashing that painful chapter of her life was unappealing at best.

She took a deep, steadying breath. "The last morning we were together, Travis, I went out to get your paper and bring it back to the house."

"I remember," he said grimly. "I was asleep and I thought I heard you in the room. I think I reached out for you. That's the last thing I remember until I heard the unmistakable sound of your car catapulting out of the driveway."

Lesley could feel a soft rise of color, and she hoped that she didn't clash with the vivid orange of the sundress. "I opened up the paper and read your comic strip. I was shocked to discover that you had used me as a model for one of your characters."

"Lily," he replied succinctly.

"Yes, of course. So I went back to the studio and read the first ten strips in that episode." She paused, trying to convey her feelings with her eyes, with her body, trying to make him understand. "I realize now that I misunderstood what I saw."

"What did you see, Lesley?" The voice was dark with some unnamed emotion, and she panicked at having to tell him about her humiliation.

"I saw...I thought you were...you were mocking me, Travis. I thought you were making fun of me. It hurt so badly that I couldn't think straight." She could feel the pain even now. "I had to leave," she whispered.

"And now," he said quietly. "What do you think now?"

She lifted her chin slightly to gaze into his eyes. They were still blank, but she could discern the faint flicker, a spark of warmth, and it gave her courage. Now was the moment to tell him that she understood and believed in his feelings for her. She must let him know that she trusted him, that she felt a oneness with him that would never let them down again.

The words stuck in her throat. The distance between them stretched into miles. If she told him that she thought he loved her, and he didn't, she would be humiliated. Perhaps his feelings for her had undergone a reversal. Perhaps he no longer felt the love that she had seen pouring out of the newspaper pages. Tears formed behind her eye-

lids as she watched the spark in Travis's eyes die an ago-
nizing death.

"I think that you love me." The words came out in a
gasp, and a small solitary tear trickled down her cheek.

"And you, Lesley. How do you feel about me?" His
voice was still even, controlled.

"Oh, Travis." The words were coming from deep inside her soul. "I love you so much that I can hardly stand
it."

He sat watching her, not smiling, not reaching out to
touch her. Then he stood up. "Prove it, Lesley."

"Prove it?" Her voice was anxious.

"Yes. That's right. I want you to prove it. I want you to
stand up on that chair, and shout to the whole damned
Roanoke airport that you love me."

Lesley looked at him, her eyes wide in shock, and for the
first time, she recognized the hurt in his answering gaze.

"I won't marry a woman who constantly feels like I'm
trying to humiliate her. I won't marry a woman who goes
through life worrying about what people are thinking of
her. I don't want you leaving me everytime you get suspicious of my motives. Prove it to me and to yourself, Lesley. Get up on that chair and tell the world that you love
me."

Travis's voice was even, but his eyes were serious.

"But Travis, I can't...I've never..." Her voice trailed off
in embarrassment.

"Do it, Lesley. If you love me, trust me. Do it," he insisted firmly.

"Be reasonable, Travis, what will this prove?" she
asked, desperation edging her voice.

"You are clearly more afraid of humiliation than anything else. I want you to embarrass yourself. Do it for me."

She stood up helplessly and he moved close to her chair
to hold out a hand. Not believing that she was actually

doing it, Lesley put one foot on the chair and with a certain lack of grace, stood on the chair in the middle of the airport terminal. People milling around nearby stopped and stared and soon there was a certain hushed expectancy in the crowd that was gathering.

She started to speak and then found that she had lost her voice. Silently she pleaded with Travis, but he merely lifted his eyebrow expectantly. With the man she loved standing below, looking up at her with respect and faith in her abilities, Lesley plunged forward.

"Ladies and gentleman," she said in a choked voice that nevertheless carried to the edge of the little crowd. "I just want to tell the world that I am in love with this man, Travis Hagen. I trust him, I admire him, and I want him. And this is the last time I go along with any crazy ideas like this!"

The crowd applauded wildly as Travis lifted her off the chair, her body sliding down his until their mouths were locked together in a kiss that both felt in every cell of their bodies. Later when the crowd had dispersed, they walked with arms tightly wrapped around each other to retrieve Lesley's luggage.

"Well, I hope that's the end of the long series of dumb things I've done since I met you, Travis." She felt his arm tighten around her.

"Well, there is one more thing. You're going to marry me, as soon as possible. But then, only an idiot would say that qualifies as dumb." Travis stopped momentarily to enjoy the blissful expression on her face. "You know, you'll never look silly to me, even when you expound from a chair in the middle of a busy airport. I thought you were the most charming, appealing, perpetually lovable woman I ever met right from the beginning."

He turned her to face him. "I loved you when you looked like this," he said pulling her hair back from her face. "And I loved you when you wore dresses down to here." He touched her leg, sending sparks flying through her body. "And I loved you when I couldn't tell what color your eyes were because of those glasses you wore."

"Why didn't you tell me, then?" she asked, needing to understand.

"I was afraid, just like you were and it took Bubba and Lily to show me the way. The day before you left I reread the series and the truth was so plain that I couldn't miss it. I'd been planning that episode for weeks, before I ever even met you...but there you and I were, staring out of the funny papers and I knew that I was hooked."

"May Bubba and Lily live happily ever after," she said.

He kissed her again, to the delight of bystanders. "And may Lesley and Travis do the same."

With luggage in hand they walked out to the parking lot. To Lesley, the Roanoke sunshine was pale in comparison to the singing brightness inside her. She was home, she was with the man she loved, and she was going to marry him. The world couldn't be any more wonderful. Life was a fairy tale come true.

She surveyed the parking lot looking for Travis's silver jeep. From the corner of her eye she saw a flash of blue and with a prickle of excitement she turned to see the ancient blue pickup truck and the old farmer sitting inside. She watched in delight as he winked at her.

"Travis," she said, turning to grasp his arm as he walked toward the other end of the lot. "There's the old farmer I've been telling you about. The one who looks like Grandpa Silas."

Travis looked over his shoulder and shrugged. "I don't see anybody, Lesley."

She spun around. The pickup and its occupant had disappeared without a trace. She gauged the physical possibility of such a disappearance. Smiling to herself she caught up with Travis. "I guess I was mistaken."

"Not about me, I hope," he countered.

"Never about you, my love. Never again about you."

# The Silhouette Cameo Tote Bag Now available for just $6.99

Handsomely designed in blue and bright pink, its stylish good looks make the Cameo Tote Bag an attractive accessory. The Cameo Tote Bag is big and roomy (13″ square), with reinforced handles and a snap-shut top. You can buy the Cameo Tote Bag for $6.99, plus $1.50 for postage and handling.

Send your name and address with check or money order for $6.99 (plus $1.50 postage and handling), a total of $8.49 to:

**Silhouette Books
120 Brighton Road
P.O. Box 5084
Clifton, NJ 07015-5084
ATTN: Tote Bag**

SIL–T–1

The Silhouette Cameo Tote Bag can be purchased pre-paid only. No charges will be accepted. Please allow 4 to 6 weeks for delivery.

Arizona and N.Y. State Residents Please Add Sales Tax

Offer not available in Canada.

*Silhouette Romance*

# COMING NEXT MONTH

### AFTER THE MUSIC—Diana Palmer
Rock singer Sabina Cane had been warned that Hamilton Thorndon was a formidable man, but nothing could have prepared her for the impact he would have on her life.

### FAMILY SECRETS—Ruth Langan
Who was blackmailing Trudy St. Martin? Caine St. Martin and Ivy Murdock joined forces to discover the culprit's identity, and in the process they discovered the secrets of love.

### THE HIGHEST TOWER—Ann Hurley
BeeGee was fearless enough to join the Greenings in their work as steeplejacks, but when her heart started falling for Dan Greening she became determined to keep her feet firmly on the ground.

### HEART SHIFT—Glenda Sands
Arson…someone had burned down Chris's shop. Chris felt lucky that handsome and imposing Ian West was on the case, until he told her that she was the prime suspect.

### THE CATNIP MAN—Barbara Turner
Julia treated life as a serious matter until, aboard a Mississippi riverboat, she met Chad. His infectious good nature chipped away at her reserve and brought laughter and love to her heart.

### MINE BY WRITE—Marie Nicole
Professor Kyle McDaniels gladly offered to help Mindy Callaghan with her writing, yet when it came to offering his heart, he was the one who needed a little help.

## AVAILABLE NOW: